the girlfriend request

JODIE ANDREFSKI

This book is a work of fiction. Names, characters, places, and incidents are the product of the author's imagination or are used fictitiously. Any resemblance to actual events, locales, or persons, living or dead, is coincidental.

Entangled Publishing, LLC
2614 South Timberline Road
Suite 109
Fort Collins, CO 80525
Visit our website at www.entangledpublishing.com.

Crush is an imprint of Entangled Publishing, LLC.

Edited by Alethea Spiridon
Cover design by Heather Howland
Cover art from Deposit Photos

Manufactured in the United States of America

First Edition January 2016

For Hope Emma. Thank you for being the most amazing daughter in the world. Never doubt how beautiful, smart, and talented you are. May you one day find love in your best friend too. I love you more than you could ever know.

Chapter One

Emma

He had 247 friends.

Now to add one more to the list.

I'd spent the last two weeks of my life carefully mapping out every piece of the plan. Forethought, strategy, research—it all came down to this very moment.

"It'll work. You can do this." I chanted encouragement to myself as the mouse hovered over the photo of a smiling, perky-looking teenage girl. I tried to ignore the small beads of sweat forming at my hairline as I stared at the photo taunting me from the screen of my Dell.

Shiny blond hair flowed over sun-kissed shoulders peeking out of a cutesy white sundress. Who the heck had hair like that unless she's in a hot pink package and distributed by Mattel?

His grinning face in an overlapping profile window caused my pulse to speed up. Like usual.

A quick *knock* sounded on my bedroom door. I

immediately tried to hit the minimize button while swiveling in my seat, just in time to see Dad poke his head in the room.

"Hey, Emma! Your mom and I just got back. How's the project coming along?"

I gulped down my surprise to see him home so soon and casually shifted the laptop's screen. "Ah...almost done."

About an hour ago I'd begged out of running to the store with my parents, using the excuse of having to finish a big project. I sort of left out the fact it wasn't exactly for school like they'd assumed.

"Do you need any help? I'm pretty good with those types of things if I do say so myself." His wide smile showed pride, and he patted himself on the chest with firm *thumps*.

"Nope, I'm good, but thanks anyway." I smiled, hoping he'd get the hint and leave so I could finish.

"If you're sure."

"I'm sure."

He waved and disappeared down the hall.

That was close. I'd die of embarrassment if either of my parents discovered what I was really up to.

As I pulled the laptop back into position, a slight *zing* of anticipation thrummed through my fingers. I resumed my study of the screen, and nerves caused my stomach to host a swarm of angry moths, making me feel slightly ill.

Before I could talk myself out of it, I hit the "request friendship" button on Eli Perry's profile.

As soon as the page showed a pop-up happily declaring the request sent, the moths went into epileptic fits. What in the world was I thinking? He'd find out. I might as well stick a big "L" on my forehead right now.

Somehow, he'd figure out that the perky Barbie lookalike who just sent him a friend request didn't even exist. I'd made up the entire Facebook profile in the hopes of starting an online friendship with Eli, which would hopefully lead to more. Like...*way more.* As in going out, full-on girlfriend more. From friend request to girlfriend—it all seemed so completely logical when I'd planned it out over the past couple of weeks, although I was starting to question that logic right about now.

My best friend Sarah thought I was nuts.

Creating the fake profile had actually been easy. God bless the Internet. The mystery girl originated from the JC Penney website, a site I figured only soccer moms ever frequented. Pretty confident Eli didn't spend much time shopping online in the JCP Juniors department, I'd felt safe swiping the photo from the section advertising the new summer clothing lines.

Aside from a cheerleading bit I'd thrown in (I could barely even do a cartwheel), it pretty much listed things that were actually true about the real me—that would be the key to gaining his interest, and making the entire plan work. "Kelli" had to be someone who liked most of the same things he did. Like, well...like *me.*

It made sense that presenting myself in a pretty, blond package instead of the ordinary one I saw in the mirror every day would be what it took to get Eli to finally notice me. Ya know, like an actual girl, complete with boobs and other girl parts, despite the fact that some guys I'd seen at the beach had more up top than I did.

Despite the motivational speeches, my stomach continued to clench like the time Carissa "accidentally" whipped a softball directly at my gut last year in gym class. Because if Eli did figure out that it was me behind the request, he'd know the secret I'd wanted to tell him for so long, and couldn't. That I liked him. I mean, *like*-liked him.

Out of habit, I smoothed my finger over a strip of photos stuck in the edge of my bulletin board. It came from one of those machines where you slip in a buck and get four small, grainy pictures fed out from the slot a few minutes later. Eli and I had scrunched together in the tiny booth, making dorky faces at the screen for three of them. On the fourth, I'd rested my head on his shoulder while he leaned against mine. His smile was content, happy. It was my favorite of the four.

I sighed, remembering the first time I saw Eli like it was yesterday. I'd been six years old and brand new to the neighborhood. He'd shuffled over, shaggy dark hair poking out from beneath the brim of his dusty Phillies baseball cap.

I'd been moping, sitting on the curb watching my parents unload box after large brown box from the giant moving truck and carrying them into our new colonial style white house. I hadn't cared a bit about the large yard, the good schools, or the pretty burgundy shutters my mom kept going on and on about. All I knew was that I didn't belong in the stupid town.

Then this strange boy reached his hand out toward me, slightly dirty fingers clutching a large yellow box of candy. "Want a Gobstopper?"

At the sound of his voice, I'd turned my head and looked up. The sun behind him made a bright halo around his grinning face, but what I remembered most about the first time I saw Eli was his eyes. They made me stare, because they weren't just one color like all the other people I'd ever known. His were green and blue and gold all swirled together, like when I made sand-art.

He waited patiently, arm outstretched, while I made up my mind. I finally nodded, whispering "Thank you," and held out my own small hand. His infectious grin grew even wider, showing off a dimple in his right cheek. He plopped down on the rounded curb next to me and shook the box, spilling several of the jawbreakers into his palm. Rooting until he found the one he was looking for, his body twisted toward me as he held out the round, cherry-colored candy like a gift. Leaning in a little closer, he whispered a bit shyly, "You can even have a red one. They're the best."

And that's when it happened. *That* was the moment I'd begun to fall for my new next-door neighbor. From that day on, we were practically inseparable, and we only grew closer through the years. He held my hand as we waited for the bus on my first day in a new school that fall, and unknowingly held my heart for each of the ten years since that hot, summer day.

But now I had a way to make Eli finally look at me as something other than his buddy, a plan to make him fall completely in love with me. Kelli's picture and my personality and words. When the time was right, I'd simply reveal the *real* person behind the profile, and we'd both laugh about it, and be so happy I was clever enough to bring us together. At least that's how I really, *really* hoped it would go down. I refused to consider any other outcome.

Chapter Two

Emma

A buzz from the side pocket of my shorts distracted me from worrying about exactly which level of stupidity I'd advanced to thanks to my latest action. I immediately panicked when I saw the name and avatar displayed on the screen of my phone.

Why was he calling? Sundays were always the same. We'd meet at Valenti's later to grab some pizza, and then head back here for our long-standing Sunday movie night.

My temples throbbed. He must have been online, seen the friend request, and somehow knew I'd sent it. The gotta-puke feeling returned.

The buzzing stopped for about ten seconds, only to start right back up again. He wasn't giving up.

Licking my dry lips, I stabbed the answer button and offered a way-too-cheery, "Hey, you! What's up?"

Deafening silence from the other end of the line.

"Eli? You there? You couldn't wait until tonight to hear my voice, right?"

A massive sucking in of breath whipped through space before his voice exploded into my right ear. "What the heck, Emma?"

Before I could say anything, he rushed on.

"*Seriously?* I can't believe you'd do this to me."

Crap, he *did* know. "I, uh, I just…"

My tongue stuck to the roof of my mouth, reminding me of the time I'd almost gagged shoving in a handful of salt-water taffy.

"You promised." His voice burned hot with accusation.

"I know. I just…" Now wait, what? What promise? I never promised not to create a fake Facebook account.

It hit like a slap to the face. "Omigod, I was supposed to feed Vader this weekend while you were gone," I whispered. Tilting my head back, I closed my eyes and slumped down in my desk chair.

The screaming silence returned. It didn't matter—the hurt accusations still managed to fly through the phone lines loud and clear. Any NSA guys listening in were probably shaking their heads at my monumental screw-up.

"I'm so sorry. I have no idea how I could have forgotten."

Because you were too busy plotting a fake online profile to try to pull one-over on your best friend in the world.

Dead air. He wasn't letting me off the hook that easily.

"Please, Eli, I'm really sorry."

Remembering that his parents had also been away on a business trip made me afraid to ask the next question. "Is he…is he okay?"

A grunt in response made me feel slightly better. Not much, but some. I was the worst friend in the world.

"Yeah, he's fine, although I can't say the same for the house. He managed to get in the pantry where I keep his dog food, rip the bag open, and eat it all. Along with half of the bag itself." He paused. "And after that, it looks like he decided to throw half of it back up all over the place downstairs. That doesn't even take into account that he made the mud room his personal litterbox."

I winced. Definitely not good. Shoving my free hand through my bangs, I slowly let out a long breath. This really wasn't a good start to my grand plan of winning his heart forever and ever.

"I really am sorry."

"I know." Another grunt. "I just don't get it, Em. I mean, you're the one that offered to do it in the first place when I told you about my trip. I could have boarded him, but you insisted you wanted to do it." Anger finally leaving his voice, he continued on quieter, with concern. "Are you okay? Did something happen?"

Here I almost starved his childhood pet, and he wanted to make sure that *I was* okay. I was going to burn in hell, no doubt about it.

"What do you mean?"

"Did that bitch on wheels do something at school Friday when I wasn't there?"

He didn't even have to say her name. I knew exactly who he meant. Carissa Kevans, the bane of my high school existence. For whatever reason, she'd made it her mission to embarrass, humiliate, or otherwise antagonize me in every way known to man. We liked to call her Carissa DeVille.

"No, it's nothing like that." Standing up, I rotated my shoulders while walking over to my bed to ease down onto its welcome softness. It felt wonderful after sitting in the hard desk chair for close to an hour.

"Look, I can tell *something's* going on. I can hear it in your voice, plus you've been acting kind of weird for like a week now." He pressed. "I thought you could tell me anything."

Yeah, except for the tiny little fact that I'm in love with you.

"Em?"

"It's nothing, I'm fine. So tell me about your weekend."

He sighed, but began to tell me stories about the other players and coaches, how they ran him ragged, how the food stank, but he still loved it anyway.

I smiled as I listened, allowing his voice to wash over me. While he talked, I stared across the room toward my bookcase. Mom and Dad had bought it for me a couple of years ago when I started high school and redid my room.

On the top shelf of honor sat several black-framed photographs of Eli and me together through the years. Red-cheeked in bright suspendered snowsuits, dragging a toboggan between us when we were about eight, covered in mud after a particularly messy homemade obstacle race at eleven or so. My favorite was the one where I sat on a swing, head tilted back in laughter. Eli held the swing's chains, looking down at me with his incredible grin, eyes shining. We'd taken it just last summer in the back yard.

"It sounds like you had a great time," I said when he finished.

"Yeah, it was pretty amazing." His voice lowered. "So you really aren't going to tell me what's going on?"

I rubbed my eyes as I tried to think what to say. I obviously couldn't tell him the truth about what had been preoccupying my mind lately, so I wimped out.

"Thanks, but honestly, everything's fine. It's probably the stress of SATs and finals coming up."

I could almost see him flop down in the obnoxious Eagles bean-bag chair in his room, Converse clad feet dangling over the side, probably tapping his fingers against his perfectly muscled leg like he so often did without realizing it. The thought made me swallow.

"So, are we still on for tonight?" I asked.

"Yep. I just have to finish cleaning up here, then get caught up on some email and we can head out. Do you want me to pick you up when I'm done or just meet there?"

"Let's meet." I glanced at my clock. "We're getting ready to head out any minute. I'll text you when I can make an escape."

"That works. Oh! And after this weekend, I get complete decision-making authority for tonight's movie selection."

I couldn't help but laugh. "Fair enough. See you in a couple hours."

"Later!" And he was gone.

Bringing my hand up toward my chest, I laid the phone against my heart, wishing it could magically communicate all the things I was too chicken to say. I closed my eyes, imagining how different life would be once my plan worked and we were a real couple.

My daydreaming came to an abrupt end when my mom poked her head in the room. "Emma! What are you doing? I told you we were leaving at two. Your dad's waiting in the car. Are you ready to go?" She fired questions at me one after the other like an automatic weapon.

She still wore her church clothes—crisp blue linen skirt, button-up blouse, hair neatly tucked into a perfect twist. Mom looked every inch the school guidance counselor she was, complete with a slightly irritated expression.

Swinging my legs over the side of the bed, I sighed. "All right, all right, I'm ready."

Her narrowed eyes held mine as she studied me for a moment. "Is everything okay?"

Standing up, I made sure to tuck my phone back into my pocket. "I'm fine. Sorry, I didn't realize what time it was. I was talking to Eli."

Next came Mom's knowing look, but she said nothing at first. Smoothing a non-existent wrinkle from the side of her skirt, she assumed a nonchalant tone. "How is he? Are you going to be seeing him later?"

My hands stilled from throwing items into a tote bag. "Well, yeah. We always get together on Sunday."

"I know." Stepping into the room, her navy pumps made no noise on the plush, lime carpet—carpet that Mom had tried her best to convince me not to select when redecorating, stating it was an eyesore and in no way conducive to rest and relaxation. Her words, not mine.

I'd won that battle, arguing it was my personal space, and that it went perfectly with the printed bedspread and curtains I'd picked out. At least my room could reflect aspects of my personality I never let come through anywhere else.

At school, I was the invisible girl. There was at least one of us in every grade, the one who silently sat in class and got As on every test but never raised her hand. I wasn't in any extra-curricular clubs, unless you counted the Math League, and no one did. Even I'd admit my clothing choices were safe, bland—and utterly boring.

By now, Mom had crossed over to stand behind me as I sat at my vanity table. She stood silently, watching me in the mirror. I rolled my eyes as I removed my hair tie, and attempted to tug a brush through my long, wild curls, despising them more with every pull. I finally gave up and slammed the brush back down on the dresser, tears threatening. I wasn't even sure what was wrong; I just felt so lost lately, like the kid sitting alone at the playground watching all the other kids play.

Gentle hands on my shoulders distracted me from the self-pity party. I sniffed back tears.

"Shh, sweetie, stop." Mom reached up and softly smoothed my hair back and began to braid. The action reminded me of when I was a little girl and she would sit behind me on my big white four-poster bed. She would sing while she twisted my hair into one smooth braid that would spill down the back of my favorite pink Belle nightgown, the one with the lace ruffle at the top that always made me feel so pretty.

Tilting my head forward slightly, I allowed her to take me back in time to the days when I still believed in fairytales and happily-ever-afters. Back to when I had complete faith that the Prince would always see that the quiet girl was really a secret Princess, and pledge his undying love before he kissed her.

As Mom's hands stilled on my back, my eyes drifted open and I once again saw the more grown-up me staring back from the mirror, and the magic disappeared. I'd stopped believing the fairytale a while ago, pretty much when I realized that the quiet, average girl didn't really get the guy. Instead, that honor went to the outgoing, perky Barbie-clones with perfect smiles who knew how to giggle and flirt to get whatever they wanted.

Finished, Mom twisted the elastic tie around the bottom. Leaning in, she hugged me from behind, meeting my gaze. "There. You look beautiful." She smiled.

Yeah, right. *Beautiful.* A mom has to say that. Some unwritten rule of motherhood.

I offered a weak smile in return. "Thanks."

My stomach twisted, because Mom's face looked worried. Even so, I could see myself in my mom's reflection—the same dark eyes, small nose, the same wide mouth, but somehow on my mother it looked elegant.

"Emma, I respect if you don't want to talk about whatever you're feeling right now. But"—she spun me around to face her before continuing—"I wish you could see yourself the way others see you. You might be surprised." Giving me another quick hug, she added, "And that includes a certain neighbor."

I pulled back and stammered, "This has nothing to do with him. I don't know what you mean."

Mom tilted her head slightly before giving a gentle smile. "Okay. Either way, you're special, Emma. Don't forget that."

Dropping her arms back down to her sides, she turned and headed to the door. "We'll be down in the car. Don't take too long."

I nodded. "I'll be right there."

She left the room, leaving me to my own thoughts. She had no idea what she was talking about; there was no way Eli could see me as anything really special. As a good friend, sure. He'd do anything for me, and always had my back, but as more than that? Something romantic? No way the thought ever occurred to him, that was for sure. Guys like him didn't go after girls like me except in movies or books. Real life wasn't that generous.

But all that was going to change. I stood, lifting my chin. No more waiting in the wings. I was ready to play the starring role in the story of my life, with Eli as my leading man.

Chapter Three

Eli

Something was up. I didn't care what Emma said, no way she was acting that weird over SATs coming up. One of the smartest people I knew, her intelligence was one of the things I admired the most about her.

I leaned back in my beanbag chair and stared outside. The sight of a piece of Emma's window, visible behind the oak tree in the yard, reminded me of the time we'd strung tin cans together and tried to use them like walkie-talkies after seeing it in some old movie. I shook my head and laughed. It hadn't worked out that great. We'd given up after about forty-five minutes of pretty much shouting across our yards to hear each other.

It'd been Em and I doing crazy stuff like that almost as far back as I could remember, ever since she moved to town. What was so great was that she wasn't like some of the other girls at school—I could just relax and be myself around her without having to worry about all the stress of relationship crap. It wasn't like that with us. My friend, Kevin, didn't get it. He kept asking me if I was "hitting that." Kevin's relationships—or should I say hookups—tended not to last past one or two nights. Me and Emma? It was different. I wouldn't change a thing.

I grabbed my laptop to upload some of the pictures to Facebook. Soccer camp had been epic. We'd learned a ton of new drills and the coaches were awesome. With the new footwork I'd picked up, we'd totally crush McKinley in the playoffs. With so many schools in the Lancaster area competing in Division I, it took a lot of sweat and hard work to earn the title, which was why it'd been so important to go to the extra training camp. Hopefully college scouts would see me this season and offer a scholarship. I wasn't supposed to know, but walls were thin. Although Mom was selling more of her work, money was still a little tight since Dad's old company downsized and he had to start consulting.

A new friend request showed pending from a Kelli Summers, but I didn't recognize the name. I clicked it open and stared. Damn, this Kelli was cute. Out of my league actually, more like someone you'd see modeling swimsuits or something. I leaned in closer to read her profile. She looked like *that* and liked Star Wars? Talk about a no-brainer. Friend request accepted.

I leaned back and smiled. Talk about a day looking up. Kind of made up for having to clean up the mess Vader made in the house.

A quick glance at the time reminded me that I'd better get a move on. I shifted in the lumpy chair, sore muscles complaining. Maybe a shower would help. I sniffed under my arms. Oh yeah, I reeked. My stomach grumbled, reminding me I hadn't eaten since before we got on the bus to head home.

I couldn't wait to hit Valenti's. Besides the fact that Em and I both loved their pizza, we made the restaurant our usual Sunday spot since it was close to where she visited her grandparents each week. Either I walked over to meet her there after her visit, or sometimes I'd drive her and stay while she visited her grandparents before we grabbed dinner before our weekly movie night.

Besides looking forward to the food, I wanted to make sure she was okay. I stood up and stretched. I'd get it out of her. After all, we'd never had secrets between us.

Chapter Four

Emma

"Bye Nana, bye Pappy. I love you!"

As I leaned in to kiss each of their softly wrinkled faces, a surge of love washed over me. Old-fashioned or not, I really enjoyed my family's tradition of visiting my grandparents at the retirement home for a few hours each week.

I'd kept surreptitiously checking my iPhone all afternoon, and knew right away when Eli hit accept on "Kelli's" friendship request. A quiver of excitement ran through me. It was starting.

Since Mom and Dad wanted to stay to watch some old movie with Nan and Pap, they'd told me I could head out and walk the three blocks to Valenti's.

Stepping out into the late afternoon air, I smiled and breathed in deeply as a rush of sun and breeze hit. April wasn't always this warm in Pennsylvania, so the recent spikes in temperature were a welcome change. Although it probably wouldn't last, it felt great to be able to throw on shorts instead of long pants and a jacket.

I didn't pay much attention to the quaint shops or the couples window shopping hand in hand as I strolled down the quiet street. My mind focused on trying to think if I'd covered my tracks. I'd waited to send the request until I had already racked up a bunch of other "friends" on Kelli's page.

It amazed me how plenty of kids, mostly guys, were more than happy to add some hot girl to their friends list even though they had absolutely no idea who she was. For all those other kids knew, I could be some creepy sixty-year-old man sitting in my underwear, typing away from my basement apartment.

Fingers of guilt crept in since I was totally pretending to be someone else too. I quickly reminded myself that I wasn't some creepo stalker; I just wanted to get a guy to fall in love with me. Okay, so maybe not completely above-board, but still.

As I rounded the street corner, red neon lettering on a building partway down the block spelled out the word PIZZA. Eli's black Jetta sat parked near the door, close to the large awning in front of the restaurant.

I smoothed my plain navy T-shirt flat against my stomach, willing the unsettled feeling in my gut to disappear. I could do this. I had a 3.8 GPA and took honors classes for crying out loud. This should be a piece of cake.

Twirling an empty straw wrapper around my index finger, I tried to think of a way to work the conversation around to Facebook. Since I didn't have much of an appetite, I'd only nibbled at the slice in front of me on the grease-streaked paper plate. Finished, I sat in the padded booth across from Eli and watched him devour his fourth slice.

The overhead fan spun lazily, seeming to push warm

rather than cooled air down on us. My bare legs stuck to the red vinyl seats. The random thought that I might have pepperoni stuck in my braces made me run my tongue over my teeth. Out of nowhere, the image of doing the same thing to Eli rushed through my head, and I couldn't help but stare at his mouth.

He glanced up to catch me studying him. "Do I have sauce on my face or something?" He absently swiped his mouth with the back of his hand.

"What? Oh, no." Warmth rushed up my neck and into my cheeks as I shook my head. "I was just thinking."

He pushed his sauce-speckled plate away and leaned in. "About?"

Yeah, I *so* wasn't telling him what had really been on my mind. I dropped the wrapper and played with the packets of sugar nested in a small white dish on the table instead.

"I don't know. A bunch of stuff. Summer vacation coming up in a couple months, how next year will be our last in high school. That kind of thing."

In one smooth movement, he reached over, took the sugar packets from my grasp, and placed them back in the container with one hand while holding my wrist gently with the other. Tiny fragments of energy sizzled against my bare skin where he touched me, kind of like the sparks that shoot out from a sparkler you played with as a kid.

His gaze was questioning. "Em, you seem nervous. I know you told me earlier that nothing was going on, and I tried my best to not bring it up for the past"—he glanced at his watch—"forty minutes."

My entire arm still tingled from even that casual touch.

As his thumb lightly brushed the inside of my wrist, I reached over without thinking and pressed my hand against his. I suddenly felt like a little kid poking at an electrical socket, knowing it probably wasn't a good idea and I might get shocked, but unable to resist. He offered an encouraging smile. "Now c'mon. Whatever's going on, stop worrying." *Ha!* If he only knew.

"You're right, summer is almost here. And you know what that means?" He grinned broadly, causing his dimple to peek out. He hated his dimple, I loved it.

Unable to resist him, I relaxed and smiled back. "No. Tell me, Yoda, what does that mean?"

"It means..." He drew out his response as he stood, pulling me up with him. "That we're going to finally get a bunch of us together to actually take that road trip to Ocean City we've been talking about for the past two years."

"Are you crazy? My parents will never let me go to the beach with a bunch of kids and no adults."

He waved away my protests. Reaching into the back pocket of his jeans, he pulled out his wallet. "Here, dinner is on me."

I fought disappointment when he released my hand to grab a twenty and throw it on the table next to the check.

"What are you doing? It's my turn. You paid last week, remember?"

"Whatever. Consider it my way of saying it's nice to be back and see you after soccer camp." He tossed me a quick grin.

"You were only gone two days, not two months." I rolled my eyes, brushing away the comment that secretly made me glow inside.

Eli tipped his head. "Okay. So consider it my way of apologizing for yelling at you earlier."

Covering my face with my hands briefly, I grimaced. "You had every right, I screwed up. And I feel awful about that."

He placed his hand on the small of my back to lead me toward the exit as he shook his head. "Doesn't matter, I overreacted. So, I'm sorry too. I know you'd never purposely break a promise you made to me. It was an accident." Pulling the glass door open, he motioned me out first, following close behind. "I know you," he reiterated as we walked toward his car. "And I know I can trust you. You'd never lie to me. It's as simple as that."

The fake profile photo flashed in my head.

I smiled weakly as he gallantly opened my car door with a flourish before jogging around to get in his own side. As he turned the key, he glanced my way. "Oh, and I hope you're ready for my movie pick."

"What'd ya get?" We took turns grabbing a movie from Redbox, and agreed to watch each other's picks—with varying degrees of success.

"It's a surprise," he teased.

Expelling a long fake sigh, I said, "Fine, but it better not be anything as bad as that one you made me watch a couple weeks ago."

He shook his head and chuckled. "*The Hills Have Eyes*? What was wrong with that one? I went for an oldie but a goodie."

"Yeah, well it had the oldie part right. Other than that, oh my God. Just...no." I wrinkled my nose.

"You screaming when they came through the trailer door. Classic." He tipped his head back, howling with laughter as he eased into a stop at a red light.

I rolled my eyes and stuck my tongue out. "So, what did you do this afternoon?"

His tan fingers lightly grasped the leather wheel, turning it slightly when the road veered left and he began moving forward again. He managed to make the simple act of driving a turn-on.

"Not much. Straightened up. Unpacked my stuff from training camp. Messed around online a little."

My heart rate sped up at the last part. "You said you were going to take pictures while you were at camp. Did you post them on your page yet?"

The wind through the open windows blew his hair forward slightly, causing it to fall into his eyes. "Yep, I took pictures. I didn't have time to get them all up, but I put a few on my page."

"Well, how about when we get back to my place we check them out before we watch the movie?" Since that might sound like it was coming out of nowhere, I hurried on in a teasing tone, "I want to see evidence you were really there, and not at some geek convention."

My actual motivation was thinking that if we went online together, he might bring up the request from Kelli, since he didn't know her. Or else I could casually bring it up since it showed in his feed that he'd added a new friend.

"Yeah, right. Like if I was at a geek convention I'd show you pictures just so I'd have to hear you calling me R2-Geek2 again for a month." Laughing, he leaned over to turn up the radio. "I love this song." He began to drum the beat out on the wheel before joining in for the chorus.

Listening to his throaty voice singing was like listening to ocean waves crash against the shore, relaxing and exciting all at the same time. I fought off a cheesy grin, and hummed along, too.

The drive home went quickly, and before I knew it, the familiar trees edging the end of our street came into view. It was hard to believe how much things changed from the first time I'd seen those towering maples. Back then I'd wanted nothing to do with this town. Now I couldn't imagine not living here, not meeting Eli. It's funny how our attitudes about life or circumstances change when we least expect it.

Streetlights hadn't come on yet since it wasn't even 7:00. Children still shrieked with laughter and yelled to each other from different yards. Calls of, "You're it!" and, "Billy, it's my turn to use the scooter!" floated our way.

A quick punch to the garage-door opener next to his visor, and Eli swung into the driveway leading up to his house. After we pulled in, the whiney rumblings of the wide door closing ushered us into an artificial darkness. It smelled vaguely of a combination of motor oil and cut wood as we sat in the parked car.

His quiet gaze caught mine. A heartbeat later, something in his look shifted. When he didn't immediately look away or say anything, I felt suddenly unsure. Something in the air between us seemed different somehow, charged.

My tongue moistened my lower lip. I became aware of what I was doing when I caught a quick movement in his throat as he swallowed, watching me. Suddenly he blinked, giving his head a half jerk.

"Umm, let me just check on Vader quick, then I'll head over to your house, okay?" His voice sounded a little higher than usual.

"Sure, okay. I'll, ah, meet you there." I stumbled over the words, anxious to get out of the car. I pulled on the door handle, grateful for the excuse to look away from the intensity of his gaze. One foot landed on the cement floor before his hand materialized on my shoulder.

"I'll be there soon," he said.

"S…see you then."

After clumsily hopping out, I strode quickly to the side door in the garage, which led to the narrow yard separating our houses.

What the heck? Things were never weird between us. I always got the familiar rush around him; I'd been dealing with that for years. But this was different.

You're just reading something that isn't there because of the whole Facebook thing.

But I couldn't get the look I thought I'd glimpsed in Eli's eyes out of my mind.

Chapter Five

Emma

Eli checking on Vader would give me maybe five minutes. I raced to my desk and opened my laptop to check for any interesting activity on my profile. Well, *Kelli's* profile.

A few messages showed unread in her inbox. It was weird, part of me wanted Eli to have an interest in Kelli, and even initiate contact with her based on the profile description I'd written. But another big part felt sick inside at the thought of him trolling for other girls.

I tried to push those feelings down, reminding myself that he needed to talk to her in order for my master plan to work. *Of course* I wanted him to talk to her.

Kinda unreal so many people would write to a total stranger with such blatant come-on lines. I actually blushed reading one of them. Anyway, nothing from the one person I wanted to hear from. *Do I message him to get the ball rolling?* Since I had nothing to lose, I decided to go for it.

Fingers poised above the keyboard, I tried to think what

to type. In any other circumstance, I would enlist Eli's help. Couldn't exactly do that now. Rotating my neck in slow circles, I considered some options.

Hey Eli!

Boring.

Hi Handsome!

Gag.

Yo Sexy!

Omigod, this so wasn't going to work. Talk about being officially clueless when it came to initiating flirting.

Finally, I settled on simple.

> *Hey! I noticed we seem to like a lot of the same things, so I just thought I'd say hi. I see you're a fan of Star Wars too. Don't laugh, but I even named my cat after a character in the movie, Princess Leia. LOL. Well, hope to talk to you soon! Kelli.*

Not great, but the best I could do. Where was my fairy godmother when I needed her advice?

Hopefully I'd managed to find the perfect blend of perky and interesting. Hopefully he wouldn't die laughing when he read it.

I'd just leaned back in my chair when footsteps bounded up the stairs. I quickly grabbed a nearby book. Eli's head poked around the doorway into my room, accompanied by a quick three-tap knock on the frame. I looked up, feigning surprise.

"Oh hey! I was reading and didn't even hear you coming up!" *Liar, liar, pants on fire!* I smiled and motioned him into the room.

He'd taken the time to comb his hair and smelled of fresh soap. I bit my lip. I should have checked my own hair. Or brushed my teeth.

I cleared my throat and swiveled around on the chair,

looking at his empty hands in confusion. "Where's the movie?"

"Oh shit! I got distracted doing some stuff, and completely forgot to grab it off my dresser."

Did the profile of a certain mystery girl distract him? My stomach flip-flopped between hope and sadness.

"Oh. Well, do you want to just run home and grab it?"

He shook his head. "Nah, that's okay. Why don't we watch something you have here?"

I scrunched my eyebrows, watching him. "You're sure?"

"Yeah, it's fine."

He walked over to where I still sat at my desk. Only inches away, he reached out his hand toward me. My breath caught until he reached past me to the computer.

"You wanted to see the pictures, right? Here, I just finished uploading the rest of them so I can show you."

As I spun in my seat to look, his breath tickled the back of my neck when he leaned in, his arm reaching around me to click the mouse. Omigod, he smelled good.

He pulled my computer closer to the edge of the desk so he could reach it better.

Oh no. I'd been logged into Kelli's account when he came over. *Kelli's account* would be open on my computer.

Bam!

I slammed the lid back down before he had it fully open, almost taking off his thumb in the process.

"What the hell?" He snatched his hand back and stared at me like I'd suddenly sprouted a second head.

I blinked. And proceeded to blurt out the first thing I could think of.

"I was bra shopping and didn't want you to see."

It was his turn to blink.

Then he looked strangled, and a sound came out of his mouth that was somewhere between a snort, a laugh, and clearing his throat. "Excuse me?"

"Bras. I was shopping for bras. You know what a bra is." I crossed my arms in front of my chest defiantly. *Bras?* What the hell was I thinking?

This time it was a clear snort. "Yes, Em. I know what a bra is. Just seems kinda strange that you'd almost remove my fingers so I didn't see a picture of one on your computer."

I scrunched my face up, thinking hard. "Well, it's different when it's a bra for me. You know, one I'll be wearing." This was getting worse by the second.

He took a quick peek at my chest, then cocked his head and stared at me.

A flush rose in my neck as he continued to study me, while I talked about bras no less. I held his gaze, refusing to say more.

Finally, he gave in. "Okay, well how about we skip the pictures and watch the movie?" His lips twitched.

Jaw set, I refused to give in to the embarrassment. "Fine," I responded, trying to sound completely cool and collected. In reality, I was praying my plush lime carpet would swallow me whole and put me out of my misery.

He reached his hand out to help me up. Taking it, I allowed him to lead me over to the bed, where we both sat down. I scooted back and sat cross-legged, spine straight. Eli, on the other hand, leaned back into a mass of pillows, looking sexy as sin.

"So, what color bra was it?" He smirked.

I refused to rise to his bait. Instead, I folded my hands primly on my lap. "So what do you want to watch?"

He stretched out even more, his six-foot frame taking up a good part of the bed. His left leg brushed against my knee. I swallowed nervously, and cleared my throat.

Eli simply gave a slow grin.

"Okay, so no help from you. How about *The Breakfast*

Club? That's always good," I said.

A *rap* sounded on the partially opened bedroom door, and my mom stepped into the room. She smiled at Eli as soon as she entered. "Eli! How was training camp? Your mom was telling me last week how excited you were to be going."

He sat up a bit, and his face reddened slightly. "Hi, Mrs. Kurtz. It was really good, thanks." It was Eli's turn to clear his throat. "I had fun and managed to pick up a couple of things that I think are really going to be helpful this coming season. We had some awesome coaches."

Mom smiled again. "I'm so glad to hear you enjoyed yourself." She turned to include me in the conversation. "Are you guys hungry at all? Do you want me to make some popcorn?"

"No, thanks, we're good. If we want anything later, I'll get it."

Given the fact that we pretty much grew up in each other's yards and homes, I knew Mom and Dad liked Eli, and more to the point, they respected him. Their only rule was that the bedroom door stayed open when he was over. Kinda funny considering nothing ever happened between us that would come remotely close to warranting a closed door.

Just then, my dad's footsteps sounded walking down the hall toward my room. "What's this? Are we having a party and you didn't invite me?" My father's attempt at being cool.

His head joined my mother's in the doorway. I began to understand how zoo animals felt. Raising my eyebrows, I looked at my parents, silently asking them to leave.

Mom seemed to get the hint. "Come on, Rob. I think there's a movie starting on Lifetime that looked good."

Dad looked stricken.

I laughed at his expression. "Have fun!"

Dad gave a final grimace before they headed down to the living room.

"A Lifetime movie, huh? I think I feel bad for your father." Eli looked at me and chuckled.

Smiling, I got brave and shifted the tiniest bit closer to him. "Don't worry, I won't make you watch one too."

"Good. Because I might not be able to recover if you revoked my man card like that."

I laughed and picked up a pillow to toss at him. "Your man card is safe with me."

He raised his eyebrows.

"Oh shut up, you know what I mean." Shaking my head, I leaned over to grab the TV remote from the nightstand. "Let's pick a movie."

"You got it." He held out his hand. As I passed him the remote, I made sure our fingers didn't touch. I couldn't handle any more shocks to the system. Plus it was critical I didn't accidentally give away how I felt about him until I was convinced that I might actually have a shot.

So, the plan was to act like he didn't affect me in the least, and get him talking to Kelli. I could do this.

Chapter Six

Eli

Today had been weird. Like, way weird.

It had to be that I was overtired from camp or something. In the car earlier when Emma had looked at me, her big brown eyes all wide and…

Uh-uh. *No way*. This was *Emma* we were talking about.

I shook my head, propped the pillow higher under me, and reached down next to my bed to grab one of my baseballs. Tossing it up and catching it a few times relaxed me. The movement followed an expected pattern—the ball goes up, the ball comes down. No weird movements you don't expect. Nothing out of left field. Simple.

But something nagged at me. I could have sworn that right before I nearly lost my fingers, I saw that Kelli chick's profile on Emma's computer.

Before I'd even had the chance to say anything about it. Why would Em be looking at Kelli's profile? It didn't make sense. Unless, of course, she'd noticed it on my timeline and was curious. That could happen. Maybe.

Regardless, my mind wasn't on Kelli. It kept going back to sitting with Em in the garage this afternoon.

Emma was pretty. Like, *really* pretty. How'd I never really noticed it before? Her wide eyes, and those full lips that just made me think of…

Argh!

I whipped the baseball across the room, knocking over a trophy on my bookshelf. What the hell was wrong with me?

I obviously needed sleep. Or maybe I needed to work out more. Or vitamins. Something.

Things with Emma and me were good just the way they were. No way I wanted to mess things up by crossing into *that* territory. I'd seen it happen with friends and the results usually ended up like crap. The people broke up and then didn't talk or else they ended up hating each other.

Kelli's profile on Emma's computer flashed in my head again. Maybe she was embarrassed to be caught looking and that's why she didn't want me to see it. But something about the profile seemed familiar and I couldn't quite place my finger on why. It was driving me nuts, since I'd never seen the girl in the photo before in my life.

I rubbed my eyes with my fists. I needed a distraction from thinking about Emma…and maybe talking to this Kelli girl would help me figure out how I knew her. If I knew her. I glanced toward Emma's house. Her room was dark. Probably sleeping already. I was the idiot awake mooning over the girl next door…how totally cliché. Emma would laugh her ass off. I sat up and reached for my laptop. I'd answer Kelli's message.

> *Hi Kelli, Nice to hear from you. I was a little surprised to get your message. You're right, it does seem like we're into a lot of the same things. Pretty cool. And really? You named your cat Princess Leia? Hmmm…*

you don't strike me as a cat person, but I could be wrong. Anyway, what did you do tonight? Anything fun? I better go, but hopefully we can talk more soon. Eli

As I leaned back against my headboard I felt nervous, almost like the time we were in the championship game and it was tie with only thirty seconds on the clock.

It wasn't very long before my computer *dinged*.

Eli, Why don't you think I seem like a cat person? Tonight I hung out with a few friends, you know, nothing too wild. Anyway, I'm glad you want to keep talking. By the way, I really liked the pictures you posted today. You look cute. =)

I smiled and ran my hand through my hair at the compliment, but a part of me felt a tiny bit let down, though I couldn't even say why. Why didn't I think she seemed like a cat person? I didn't allow myself to answer the question.

She was showing in my list of chat contacts, so I decided to send her an instant message.

Hi

She didn't answer. I frowned, and tried again.

You there?

Finally I could see her typing back, and relaxed a little.

Hi back.

So you think I looked cute, huh? I couldn't help but grin.

LOL, Yes I did. So, what did YOU do tonight? Anything fun?

Should I say I spent the evening with Emma? Would that make another girl jealous? I ran my hand through my hair again. The whole thing was starting to get confusing.

I settled for,

I'm glad you liked the photos. And yeah, I had a lot of fun tonight. Watched The Breakfast Club.

Oh, I love that movie!

The Breakfast Club was one of Emma's favorite movies too.

We talked for almost a half an hour. General *get to know you* kind of stuff at first. I finally got brave and told her how cute she was, and asked what it was about my profile that had caught her attention.

Maybe it's those mesmerizing eyes.

I almost fell out of my chair.

Before I could type a response, she changed the subject, almost like she wished she hadn't said it, so I played along. We spent five minutes discussing the pros and cons of the latest zombie series we were both addicted to instead.

Once when I got up to grab some water, I could've sworn a faint light glowed inside Emma's room, almost like she was on her laptop, too.

The more we talked, the more an idea took root in my head. What if Kelli and Emma were the same person? I told myself I was being ridiculous—wishful thinking and lack of sleep on my part. But little things she said sounded so familiar, so much like Emma, that I couldn't completely shake the thought.

About twenty minutes later, she abruptly ended the conversation.

Well, I better get going. I need my beauty rest you know.

I remembered Emma in the garage. Her dark hair spilling down her shoulders. Her wide eyes.

I responded,

No, you don't. You're beautiful just the way you are. Goodnight.

And before I could wimp out, or second guess myself, I logged off. I knew, even if my hunch was wrong, that I hadn't intended my message for the girl in the profile photo. I'd meant it for my best friend, for Emma, my girl next door.

Chapter Seven

Emma

The next few days passed in a boring blur. School, homework, eat, sleep, repeat. I'd messaged Eli twice, but hadn't heard back. Or rather, Kelli messaged Eli. The communication blackout wasn't helping my plan. On top of that, Eli seemed busy avoiding me, too. The real me.

I needed to step up my game. Only problem…I wasn't quite sure how to do that. Not exactly being the queen of flirtation made the whole thing a tad more difficult. Time to call for back-up reinforcement.

"Sarah? It's me."

"Hey girlie! What's shaking?" Sarah's voice sounded as cheerful as ever.

I leaned back on my bed, staring at the photos on my bookshelf.

"I need your help."

"Please tell me this isn't about your little plan." Now she just sounded tired and worried, the sunshine gone.

I picked at a piece of string on the sleeve of my hoodie.

"He hasn't answered since that first night. I don't know what I did wrong."

"You mean other than pretending to be someone you aren't?"

"Yeah, besides that." I chewed on the drawstring.

"And?"

"And what?"

"And has he mentioned any of this to you?" She cleared her throat. "I mean to the *real* you?"

"No. Nothing. He's not going out of his way to speak to me, either." I paused. "To be honest, we've barely talked at all the past three days. Every time I see him in the halls, he just gives me this weird look, then hurries off the other way. Or else kind of waves, and makes an excuse that he's late for something." I paused. "Do you think he somehow figured it's really me and he's avoiding me?"

Silence.

"Oh no, you do."

I wanted to throw up. Maybe I could convince my parents to move, like, to Argentina.

Sarah's supportive best friend gene must have kicked in, because she rushed on with comforting noises. "No. *No!* I'm sure that isn't it. Maybe he's really busy getting ready for finals and stuff. I'm sure it has nothing to do with you."

I *harrumphed*, not entirely convinced. "Well, you have to help me. What do I do now?"

"What did you say in your messages to him?"

"I don't know. General stuff. Kind of flirty I guess."

Sarah snorted.

I pulled my hood up, wanting to hide even though she couldn't see me.

"Okay, fine. So I just asked him some questions about himself, and told him I thought he was cute, and… I don't remember exactly."

I did remember, but couldn't bring myself to tell her how I'd called his eyes mesmerizing. Maybe that *was* a little over the top. I covered my face with a pillow. Argentina it is.

"Em. Calm down. We can still salvage this. Is he ever online when you are? Have you tried to instant message him and ask him what's up?"

"I haven't seen him on since then, but it shows he's read my messages," I muttered under the pillow.

"Okay, so that makes it a little more challenging, but still doable." She paused for a minute, obviously thinking. "Oh! I've got it!" She sounded excited now. "Why don't you suggest talking on the phone?"

I removed the pillow. "Oh, that's brilliant, because he won't recognize my voice or phone number."

"Oh ye of little faith. We'll get someone else to make the call."

I bolted upright. "Are you kidding me? No way! I'm not telling anyone else about this. It would be beyond embarrassing!"

"Oh, and it wouldn't be embarrassing if he suspects it's you and keeps playing the avoidance game?"

She had a point.

"Okay, true." I glanced out the window, trying to spot him. He was nowhere in sight. "But I wouldn't want it to be anyone that he's friends with, or that would blab about it."

"Well, obviously."

"So who do you think we should ask?" Resigned to having to enlist even more help, I couldn't believe how staggeringly poorly my plan was unfolding.

"We?"

"We." I said firmly. "Or rather, you?"

Sarah sighed.

"Please?" I drug out the word for a full three seconds.

"Well, shit. Fine. Let me think about it, and I'll call you back."

I squealed. "Thank you, thank you!"

"You owe me." She hung up without waiting for a response.

If this plan worked, I definitely would owe her, big time. I smiled in excitement.

A couple hours later as I rinsed plates to load in the dishwasher after dinner, Sarah called me back.

"Hello?" I turned off the faucet so I could hear her better.

"Okay, so what do you think about asking Mallory?"

I groaned. Mallory was this quiet mouse of a girl from my AP Science class, not at all what I imagined when I thought of the perfect girl to flirt her way into winning Eli's heart.

"Hang on a sec."

My parents were watching television in the living room, so I headed to my bedroom where I could talk without them overhearing. As I took the steps two at a time, I wondered if having someone call Eli was really the best idea. It seemed like my plan was starting to spin out of control.

After closing my bedroom door, and clicking on the desk lamp, I sat down and reflexively booted up my computer.

"Hellooo?" Sarah sounded impatient.

"Sorry, I'm here. Hang on, I wanted to check and see if he wrote back yet. Maybe we don't really have to do the phone call thing."

One quick check told me he hadn't responded, but my list of online contacts raised my hopes a bit.

"He's on!" I hissed into the phone.

"Now?"

"Yes, now." I whispered.

"Why are you whispering?"

"Because…" I stopped. "I don't know." I spoke in a normal volume. "Should I send him an IM?"

What would I even say? I pretty much sucked the last time I tried that route, and that was before the three days of incommunicado. My foot tapped nervously on the floor.

"Well?" I pressed. "Should I?"

"Sure. Maybe he'll tell you why he hasn't gotten back to you yet. I mean to Kelli." She sighed. "Seriously, you don't realize how ridiculous this whole thing is?"

I didn't answer right away, my focus a laser on his name in my contact list.

"Hello?"

"I'm here. What do I say?"

"I don't know, maybe say…" She paused. "Em, are you sure you want to do this? Keep this up, I mean?"

A big part of me wondered the same thing. Maybe I should give it up while I was ahead. Or, at least not behind. But before I could answer her, a message popped up on my screen.

Hey there.

My eyes widened at the two simple words.

"He just sent me a message." My panic rose to dangerous levels.

"He did? What did it say?"

"Hey there."

"Well, what did you say?" Sarah sounded excited now.

"Nothing! What am I supposed to say?"

"Girl, that's up to you. You know my stance on the whole thing, but you do what you gotta do."

"Gee, thanks a lot."

"What are best friends for? Look, I have to go. I'm supposed to be finishing my history paper. Let me know how it goes, okay?"

I sighed. "Okay, thanks. Talk to you later."

"See ya."

Eli's message on the screen mocked me. Deciding that I might as well answer, I typed back a simple, *hi* then watched as the box showed him typing.

Sorry I didn't have a chance to get back to you before this.

Not a problem. How have you been?

Wow, I was on fire in the flirting skills department. I wondered what he'd say. Busy? Confused? On a quest to ignore his best friend?

Pretty good, how about you?

Well, that was generic. I decided to play along.

Good, thanks.

I paused, thinking how to shift the conversation out of polite pleasantries and into something more significant. He didn't give me the time.

I didn't mean to ignore you or anything.

Before I could come up with a response, a *knock* sounded on my door, right before the knob turned. I quickly logged off and swiveled around in my chair just as my mom poked her head in the room. Not for the first time, I wished my parents would learn to wait until I said, "Come in."

"Hey sweetie, I'm sorry to bother you, but can you come downstairs and give me a hand with something?"

I smiled weakly. "Sure, Mom. I'll be right there."

Silently frustrated, I stood up and followed her downstairs. It turned out she wanted my help moving some furniture around. Dad had left for a meeting, and Mom being Mom decided she wanted to rearrange the living room. This happened a couple times a year in our house.

Almost an hour passed before we finished. By the time I got back to my room, Eli had logged off.

Probably just as well since it was late, and I still had to finish an essay for my Creative Writing class. The assignment was "An Impact." Ms. Clark loved being vague. I sighed and stared at the blank screen in front of me.

Obviously, various people had influenced my life in different ways—my parents, Eli, friends, even people like Carissa. And the move sure made an impact on my life. But it seemed superfluous just writing about the obvious.

Maybe I was looking at it all wrong. Maybe instead of simply writing about things or people around me, I should do what all my teachers kept going on and on about and look inside myself. I looked something up online, then began to type.

MAKING AN IMPACT

"As human beings, our greatness lies not so much in being able to remake the world—that is the myth of the atomic age—as in being able to remake ourselves." ~Gandhi

So often, in my most private of moments, and thinking of my reasons for being here on this earth, I am left with feeling… I just want to have made some kind of impact.

I wrote steadily for the next thirty minutes. When I finished, I read back over the words I'd written. Whether or not it was what the teacher was looking for I had no idea, but I was happy with it.

Lately I'd felt as though I was somehow losing myself, or didn't even know who I really was. It was nice to get some of those thoughts and feelings out. I'd always loved to write, had even thought about majoring in it in college. Somehow, I'd gotten away from writing, and it felt good to do it again.

Chapter Eight

Emma

"Hey, loser."

I slammed the slate metal locker closed with resignation and turned to see my least favorite person in the world.

"Carissa." I nodded tightly and moved to step past her.

Carissa stood in the middle of the junior hallway while football-playing toadies hovered on either side of her petite, Aeropostle-packaged body. Unfortunately, because of the spelling of our last names, we'd been placed in the same homeroom since ninth grade. This meant our lockers were close to each other, and we shared lunch periods. And due to Carissa's shining personality, any interaction was pretty much hell.

She'd once been human, back in elementary and middle school. She'd even gone out with Eli back in the day. Back when *going out* meant you didn't actually go anywhere, but passed each other notes in the hall between classes. Back when, if you were really lucky, you got to play seven minutes in heaven with an amazing guy at a birthday party.

In eighth grade, Carissa got really lucky at Carey Winchester's birthday party. I remember being devastated. She'd pulled Eli's name out of the hat to go in the closet together. They went out for three months after that. Then she got boobs and all the boys noticed her and it went downhill from there. She dumped Eli for a linebacker named Brad. It was her loss, and I think she knew it.

As I attempted to step around the queen of the bitch squad, she extended a foot in my path. I hurtled forward, books and binders slipping from my grasp on the way down. I would have nose-dived onto the smooth hallway floor had it not been for a pair of firm hands suddenly grasping my upper arms, preventing my spectacular dive into complete humiliation.

Grateful for the save, I raised my eyes. Eli looked straight back at me, concern etched in his features.

"You okay?" he asked quietly.

Embarrassed, I nodded. I shoved the hair out of my face and did my best to straighten the band that was supposed to be holding it back.

Eli bent and helped me pick up the dropped books with a sympathetic smile.

"Thanks," I whispered.

After handing them back to me, he turned an angry gaze on Carissa, who still stood close by, smirking. She twirled a long strand of hair around her finger, one eyebrow raised in challenge. He took two steps toward her. The fury in his gaze caused her to stop twirling and back up slightly toward the opposite wall. His usually calm face twisted in distaste.

"You know, Carissa, you've done this kind of crap to anyone you felt like for years now." Another step closer. "And you know what I think? I think you do it because deep down, you know that this is it." He motioned to the crowd around her. "This is going to be the height of your existence and it's already starting to diminish little by little. Your mommy and daddy may give you anything you want, but you're still unhappy and have to treat everyone else like garbage to feel better about yourself."

Carissa's smirk began to fade. She tried to cover by quickly adopting a haughty sneer and attempted to turn away, muttering, "Whatever."

Eli grabbed her arm as she spun away, not hard, but enough to halt her grand exit. He leaned in closer and whispered, "It's over, Carissa. You mess with Emma again, and I'll tell everyone about your little trips to fat camp."

Her blue eyes widened.

His expression didn't change.

She had the guppy look down pat. Her mouth opened and closed, but nothing came out.

Eli reached over to take my elbow and lead me away from the small group.

"Fat camp?" I whispered as we walked past Mr. Elliot's science classroom.

He laughed under his breath. "I have no idea. It was the first thing I could think of."

Laughter bubbled up as I realized he'd just completely made up the one insult that Carissa would take to heart. Being the self-appointed princess of the school's Beautiful People, she obviously wouldn't want anyone to think she ever battled something as demeaning as an unsightly bulge.

"You're awful."

"Yeah, probably, but I'm sick of the way she treats people. And no one ever stands up to her."

Conversation halted when I reached my first period English classroom. Before I went in the door, he squeezed my arm and offered an encouraging smile. "Don't listen to her, Em. She's not worth it."

"Thanks." I smiled back. Other students shoved to get past us since the bell was going to ring any minute, and Ms. Myers didn't tolerate anyone being late. I wished we were alone. Instead I said, "I better go in."

"I'll see you later, okay?" His eyes looked super blue, with only hints of green, probably from the navy fitted tee he wore under his open flannel shirt.

"Sure, see you later."

After I walked into the classroom and headed to my desk, I glanced around. Other students talked to their friends, or tried to get one last text in before class started. Myers also had a zero-tolerance policy on any type of electronics to which she rigidly adhered.

A few kids still stood around in small groups, while others sat at their desks talking to their neighbors. No one paid any attention to me when I slipped in my seat and took out my English textbook.

The bell rang, announcing the start of first period. Sighing, I flipped open my notebook and took the cap off my ballpoint pen.

8:00 a.m.

Just another day in teen paradise.

After forty-seven minutes of listening to my teacher drone on about the lesser-known themes in *Hamlet*, I was more than ready to head across the hall to Calculus. It was amazing how an instructor could take what was normally a favorite subject and turn it into a lesson in torture by boredom.

As I stood up, a flash outside the window caught my attention. Glancing over, I did a double take. Eli stood outside holding up an open notebook with the words *MEET ME NOW!!!* written in what looked like black Sharpie.

I shook my head vehemently. No way was I going to cut class. My luck, I'd get caught and land in detention.

He nodded his head up and down and pointed back and forth between the sign and me.

Checking to see if Ms. Myers saw what was going on, relief rushed through me when it appeared that she hadn't noticed a thing. She was too busy arguing with Jared Stephens over what sounded like a long-running battle over why his wrestling shorts weren't acceptable classroom attire.

Eli had now assumed a pathetically bad puppy-dog expression to go along with clasped, begging hands.

I stifled a giggle. Giving in, I nodded and held up my index finger to let him know I would be there in a minute. He gave me a thumbs-up and waved.

Walking down the hall in the opposite direction of my second period math class, I tried to appear nonchalant. All I needed was for one teacher to ask where I was going and the word vomit would spew, telling anyone within earshot how I'd been on my way to leave school without permission.

Thankfully, no one asked. Not one person seemed to notice. In times like this, invisibility had its perks.

I finally reached the end of the hall and approached a green door marked Maintenance Exit Only that led outside. I figured it was better to make my escape here, rather than using the main entrance near the offices. I couldn't chance my mother seeing me.

The bell rang for the start of the period, and I jumped. My hand flew to my chest, and I willed my heart rate to settle as I double-checked to make sure that no one noticed my big act of rebellion.

Now or never.

I pushed against the silver bar running the width of the door. Surprisingly, it opened without setting off any kind of alarm. The hinges swung soundlessly, ushering in bright morning light and fresh air.

Cat burglars had nothing on me. I slipped through all stealthy-like, half-expecting Eli to jump out and try to scare me.

He didn't.

As a matter of fact, I didn't see him *or* his damn sign.

I looked around, scanning the area. Nothing. I bit my lip as I gingerly allowed the heavy door to close behind me. My adventure gene began to recede. As I took a few timid steps toward where I'd last seen him, I called out in a stage whisper, "Eli? Where are you?"

No answer.

A few more steps.

The whispers got a little louder. "Eli, I mean it. I left school for this. You better be here or I'm going to kill you."

Just as I'd given up and was about to try to head back into the school, he pulled up to the curb at the end of the teacher's lot, right on the other side of the grassy quad where I half-crouched like some animal.

He waved me over through the open window.

"Eli!" I hissed. "Are you crazy? What are you doing? Someone's gonna see you."

He motioned again for me to join him. "Then hurry up and get in before we get caught."

Oh for…

He was nuts, which probably made me just as insane, since I did some weird crab run to try to stay out of sight while I made my way to his car.

"'Atta girl," he said after I slipped inside. Continuing to crouch down, I grabbed a pair of sunglasses from the bucket space between our seats and slapped them on, trying to hide my face the best I could.

Eli cracked up, but said nothing.

"What are we doing?" I whispered.

"Ah," he replied, unable to hide his grin. "*That*, my dear, is the surprise."

"Getting detention together?" I smirked.

He rolled his eyes.

I shoved my books and bag down by my feet, then shifted to face him. "Eli?" I asked in a warning tone.

"Shh…" He reached out and placed a finger in front of my lips to stop me from talking. "You'll find out. Just relax." He winked.

What the…

He shifted the car and hit the gas. My head flew forward a few inches from the unexpected movement, before whipping back and banging against the headrest.

I opened my mouth to yell at him to slow down, but he was already shaking his head and making *tut-tut* noises. "No complaining. And no questions about what we're doing. That's the deal."

"Why do I feel like I'm on a really bad game show?" I muttered.

Right before we pulled out of the school's parking lot, he coasted to the side of the road and looked at me.

"So, Em. I say we just do this and go have fun. Deal?" His eyes dared me to say no.

I may be a coward with some things, but I'd never backed out on a dare from him, and he knew it. I started to laugh. Bagging class and taking off was too crazy for words—and exactly what I needed. Tipping my head back, I reached up to pull the headband out, and shook my head side to side to free my hair to blow in the spring wind.

"You've got yourself a deal." I stuck out my hand.

He smiled wide, clearly pleased. He wrapped his hand around mine to shake on it. "You won't regret it, I promise."

"Well, if you promise…"

He grinned and reached out his pinkie. I did likewise, and

we did the pinky-kiss we'd done a thousand times growing up. As our pinkies locked, we both leaned in to kiss our own clasped hand, his eyes inches away from my own as we did so. My stomach fluttered as the image of kissing him for real filled my mind. I quickly pulled my hand free and backed away, clearing my throat.

Brows scrunched together, he shot me a look.

"Um…what are we waiting for? Let's go." I pasted on what I hoped passed for a normal smile, not an *I was just imagining jumping on your lap* leer.

He tilted his head toward mine. "Your wish is my command."

Unfortunately, *his* smile looked completely normal.

Sigh.

Chapter Nine

Eli

"Just tell me."

"For the tenth time, you'll see." Patience wasn't really Em's strong suit. It was kind of adorable how she kept asking for hints on where we were headed, but I wanted to surprise her.

The past few days had been a bit awkward trying to figure out if Kelli was Emma and how I felt about that if she was. How I felt about my new strange feelings about Em. Was I willing to risk our friendship to try to take things to the next level? So at first I'd taken the wuss way out and kind of avoided her, but I'd decided I wanted to try it. Em was more than worth going to bat for, win or lose.

I tapped a drumbeat out on the wheel, and glanced over as she reached down to adjust her seat for the third time. I fought back a chuckle. "You hungry?"

She looked up. "Not really. Why? Are you?"

"I could eat."

"So let's stop and you can get something. Unless we're close to where we're going?" she tacked on, obviously still hoping to get a hint.

I flashed a grin. "Nice try."

Her lips turned down in a sexy pout. I tried not to stare and pulled my attention back to the road instead. I cleared my throat.

"I saw a sign for a gas station at the next exit. I need to fill-up anyway, so I can grab something while we're there."

She didn't say anything. Was she mad at me? I thought she'd be happy about taking the road trip together. Or that maybe she'd get a clue by the status I'd posted this morning.

The more I thought about it after we'd talked so much that first night, or rather, after *Kelli* and I had talked so much, I thought maybe…that it was kind of a game. I knew Em better than I knew anyone, the way she said things, little things about her. And I picked up on those same things talking to Kelli, too.

I figured we both knew and were having fun with it, so I'd posted a smiley face this morning when I'd decided to ask her to take the trip together. But now…I wasn't so sure.

Was I completely off-base with the whole thing? What if I was the world's biggest moron and didn't even realize it?

I glanced over. She sat close to the window, her excitement from earlier seeming to have faded. I frowned. The wind blew her hair across her face, and I couldn't see her expression.

I reached over, hesitantly, and tapped her knee. "Hey, you okay?"

She didn't answer right away.

My stomach dropped. "Em?"

She played with the braided silver ring she always wore on her right hand and looked up. "Sorry, I'm fine. Ignore me. I think the whole skipping out early just has me nervous." She reached over and poked my shoulder. "But I don't want to ruin the day, so no more worrying." She crossed her heart with her finger and smiled. "I promise."

Some of the tension left my body. I reached over to take her hand and squeezed. "If you want to go back, we can." I didn't want to let go of her hand. It felt right, like it belonged there.

"No! No, I don't, honest."

"Okay, if you're sure."

"I'm very sure." She nodded and smiled again.

"Good." I gave her hand one final squeeze before reluctantly releasing and reaching over to press the track button on the CD player. "In that case, in the spirit of having fun, this song is for us." I wiggled my eyebrows and grinned.

The song was another part of my surprise. She'd know what it meant the second she heard it.

She cocked her head and waited for it to begin. When it did, her eyes widened.

"Did you pick this one for a reason?" she asked over the opening guitar.

I just grinned some more as the upbeat Yellowcard song filled the car.

"There's a place off Ocean Avenue, where I used to sit and talk to you."

She stared. "Eli! We aren't."

Music poured out of the speakers. I moved my head in time to the beat, and couldn't stop smiling at her expression.

"Ummm…yes, we are." I laughed.

She squealed, "Seriously?"

I laughed some more at her enthusiasm. I knew she'd love it. Hell, I loved it. A trip to the beach, just the two of us. The past year or so, we'd played this song over and over while we talked about taking off to spend a couple of days hanging out in Ocean City.

We'd even made a playlist of all the songs we'd listen to

on the drive. *Ocean Avenue* was first on the list.

"But wait! I thought we talked about going with a bunch of kids?"

"We will. This is just a day trip for us. We're still definitely doing the group trip this summer or Kev would kill me." I laughed then glanced at the clock on the dashboard. "So, I figure we'll get there about noon, hang out a while, and head back about five. Sound good?"

I chuckled as Emma jumped up and down in her seat like a little kid. I realized that it made me feel good inside to make her happy.

She turned to me suddenly, face stricken. "I'll have to call my parents. If I'm not home after school they'll wonder where I'm at."

I nodded. "Yeah, I know. Me too." I tapped my fingers on the wheel. "But I figure if we call when we get there, they won't be too ticked, it's not like we make a habit of ditching school."

Although she nodded, I could see she wasn't completely convinced that they'd just be cool with it.

"Or, we could tell them that we're gonna stay after school to work on some project, and say we have plans to meet Kevin and Sarah or whoever for dinner after that." I glanced her way. "Whaddya think?"

She shook her head. "I don't know."

I turned the music down a little. "It's your call. We'll do whatever you want."

She tucked her legs up beneath her on the seat. "I'm thinking we should go with option two."

"Okay. But look, if you decide you want to tell them where we really are, we can do that, too." Even as I said it, I didn't think that was the way to go. I knew her parents.

"Let's just wait and see what we think later. But for now"—she reached over and pressed the volume on the radio, turning it back up—"let's have fun." She smiled, and her whole face lit up, knocking the breath right out of me.

That's it. Now or never. I had to find out one way or the other. I really believed my hunch about the profile was right, and hoped if I brought it up, she'd admit it and we could move forward. Because I realized that the girl I wanted…the girl I'd been waiting for without even realizing it…was right next door all along. And I didn't want to wait one more day to be with her.

I took a deep breath and faced her, unable to hold back my huge smile.

"I have to tell you something," I blurted.

Chapter Ten

Emma

Eli looked ready to explode from excitement.

"Ye-es?" I prompted him.

He looked at me like I should somehow know what he was going to say next. Color me clueless because I had no idea.

My heart nearly stopped when he followed that announcement with three little words.

"I met someone."

Immediate nausea. I quickly reminded my psycho-jealous self that this was my plan, I wanted him talking to Kelli. Unless, wait…what if he meant he met *someone else*? And that's why he hadn't been answering Kelli?

I pasted on an Oscar-worthy surprised look, and merely responded, "Oh?" Like it was no big deal. I purposely raised my eyebrows slightly, and cocked my head just a tad to the right. Those body language hints I learned in psych class were finally being put to good use.

He tossed a quick glance my way, and flicked on the turn signal. "Yeah." A brief smile and nod. "I've gotta get gas. Plus I want to see what they have to eat. Maybe they sell those giant hot dogs."

Hot dogs? We were seriously discussing *hot dogs* right now?

I grimaced. "You do realize how bad they are for you, right? I mean, we've had this discussion before." My mind screamed, *Let's get back to who you met!*

Pulling into the lot of a large Sheetz, which served as a gas station and mini-mart, he waved off my comments about the dangers of eating recycled animal parts. "Don't even bother. I don't care if they *are* made of hooves and eyeballs like you always tell me. They still taste good."

I gagged.

"Hey, you don't have to eat them." He flicked me on the leg. "So can it."

"Fine, whatever. So…tell me about this girl."

Turning the car off, he shot me a mysterious look. "I didn't say it was a girl."

I snorted. "Oh please, unless you decided to switch teams, I don't think you'd feel the need to throw it out there about meeting some guy." I rolled my eyes.

He burst into laughter. "No. You're right. It's a girl." He paused and pushed his sunglasses up on his head, dark hair poking out around the tinted lenses. "It's weird. She messaged me out of the blue the other day on Facebook."

So, he *was* talking about Kelli. Good. But since in any other scenario I'd be teasing him like mad right about then, I had to stay true to form.

"Facebook? You met her on Facebook?" I wrinkled my nose. *Wait! Was that too much?*

He just stared at me.

Time to shift gears. Nodding like this was all news to me;

I tried my best to project innocent curiosity. "Huh, okay. So, what's she like?" I was half-afraid to hear his answer.

"She's…" He pressed his lips together, considering. "Let me get the gas quick while I try to figure out how to answer that." He smiled.

"Oh. Sure. Okay." The bobble-head nod returned.

As he got out of the car, he turned to face me. "Do you want anything?"

Yes! I want you to answer me! I want you to fall in love with me! But since I'm a chicken, I settled for a weak, "No, I'm good, thanks."

"All right. Be right back." He shut the door and walked toward the mini-mart.

Pushing my bangs out of my face, I bounced my head off the back of my seat several times in a row. *Think, think, think*. What would he say about Kelli? What was *I* supposed to say?

A buzz sounded, temporarily distracting me from my frantic thoughts. I reached down and rooted through the canvas bag until I found my iPhone.

I glanced at it, then inhaled sharply. It was a Facebook message notification. From Eli. *To Kelli!* A message he'd just sent.

A sinking feeling formed in the pit of my stomach. The whole trip was clearly only a means for him to ask for advice on the new girl he had the hots for. It had nothing to do with wanting to cheer me up after the scene in the hall this morning like I'd hoped.

Why was it bothering me so much that he wanted to talk to Kelli?

I quickly looked up and searched for a sign of him. All clear. Just a few college age kids laughing and stumbling out of the store with large coffees in hand.

I went back to the message.

Just wanted to say hi! Hope you're having a good day so far. I meant to ask, what made you message me in the first place? I mean, I know you said about common interests, but there has to be a ton of guys who like that stuff too. Don't get me wrong, I'm really glad you did. Guess I was just curious. Until soon, E.

Gnawing on my bottom lip, I tried to figure out what to say, how to put into words that I messaged him because he makes me smile, even when I'm having a bad day. Because he always holds my door. Because whenever there's only one handful of popcorn left, he gives it to me, and he knows what kind of ice cream to order for me without having to ask. Because he laughs at my corny jokes, and knows when I need a hug without me saying a word.

As I thought of all the reasons I'd fallen for him, a smile crossed my lips, remembering…because he gave me the cherry gobstopper all those years ago. But I couldn't say any of that.

When I began to type, my first line almost said, "Supersized to heart from you." Freaking autocorrect.

Surprised to hear from you. But def a nice surprise. =) I decided to message you that first time because you seemed different from the other guys I know. In a really good way.

Crap! He was coming.

I poked the send button, even though I'd been planning to say more. As I reached down for my bag so I could toss the phone back inside, the strap caught on something under the seat, lodging the messenger bag tightly underneath.

Dammit.

I tugged again.

He was almost around the car, coming to stand on my

side to pump the gas. Offering a big grin, he triumphantly waved a partially eaten foot-long hot dog in the air. Tucked under his other arm were two water bottles.

Unable to work the bag loose, I finally wedged the phone underneath my legs, making sure it didn't peek out from the side of my shorts. The edges dug into the very top of my thighs, making me feel like I was hatching an egg. Why didn't I just act like I'd been texting Sarah or something? But it was too late now to do anything about it. I'd look even more ridiculous pulling it out in front of him.

Just as I was cursing myself for being so stupid, he leaned down toward my window to hand me the water bottles. "I grabbed one for you, too, just in case."

"Uh…thanks." I smiled feebly, brutally aware of the phone beginning to slip between my legs as I reached out to retrieve the drinks. He'd see it pop through my thighs if it moved any more. Slightly embarrassing.

He shot me a strange look. "You okay?"

Could he tell? It was all I could do to choke back a snort, "Yep. Good to go."

Just hatching an iPhone, nothing to see here. I could barely keep my insane laughter from bubbling out.

He eyed me quizzically as he took a giant bite of his food. Chewing thoughtfully, he shook his head. Still watching me, he took another big bite.

I shifted uncomfortably in the seat. My movement must have caused me to press some button on the phone, because it suddenly made a strange sound, almost like I was farting. My eyes widened, cheeks burning. This had to be one of those weird dreams, like the kind where you show up naked at school.

"Do you have to go to the bathroom or something?" he asked calmly while still chewing.

"What? No!" Wrinkling my nose, I vehemently shook my

head as I stared at him, aghast. I could see pieces of partially chewed hotdog and bun. Not his best look.

"Okay. Just checking. You're wiggling around weird like you have to pee." Shoving the last of the hotdog in his mouth in one gigantic bite, he turned to flip the lever on the pump. He reached out to open the gas tank, and began fueling.

He craned his neck toward me and called out, "What time is it anyway?"

I glanced at the dash, but no time was visible since he had turned the car off. "I don't know. You have the keys, so I can't see."

He reached his free hand into a side pocket and pulled out his phone. After he looked at the screen, I couldn't help but notice a tiny smile cross his face before he slid it back in his jeans.

He must have read Kelli's message. But he didn't press any buttons. Maybe he just saw that she wrote back. How nice that it made him so happy.

"So, what time is it?"

"Oh, umm, quarter of eleven. We'll definitely be there by noon." He swiveled his upper body to replace the pump while he used his other hand to tighten the gas cap and flip the small door closed. "Alrighty! We're good to go."

Even pumping gas, he attracted my attention. Those muscles, those damn muscles.

He hopped back in the driver's seat, and proceeded to reach over and grab one of the water bottles, twisting the cap off before taking a long drink. After easily finishing half his water, he lowered the bottle and absently wiped his mouth with the back of his hand. "All set?" A drop of moisture clung to his bottom lip.

I nodded, trying not to stare.

He held my gaze for a moment, and then slowly replaced the cap on the bottle before he set it back in the cup holder and turned the key in the ignition. As he reached over to fasten his seat belt, he paused and looked at me again.

I watched him curiously.

One quick movement and he raised himself off the seat slightly so he could grab the phone out of his pocket. "I wanna check something."

He swiped his screen and sat quietly for a second, reading. When he was done, a ghost of a smile passed his lips as he set the phone in the space between us. Whistling now, he proceeded to buckle up and shift into drive.

Apparently, we had to play this his way.

I gave him a probing look. "Soooo…"

"I just heard from her again."

"And?" It was like pulling teeth.

"And, I don't know. She's really nice."

Nice. The death sentence for wannabe girlfriends everywhere.

"She doesn't live too far from me. I think I'm going to ask her out." He grinned, then raised his eyebrows like he was waiting for me to say something.

Wait. No. He couldn't ask Kelli out already! It wasn't time for the big reveal yet. It was way too soon.

"Are you sure you want to do that? I mean, how much do you know about this girl considering she doesn't even go to our school and you've only messaged her two times?"

"How do *you* know where she goes to school?"

"Oh. Well, I mean, I just assumed since you said you just met her. And uh, if she went to our school you would have met her before you just met her." Dear God, I had diarrhea of the mouth and sounded like a moron.

He shot me an inquiring look, his eyebrows raised and nose wrinkled.

But I couldn't be stopped. I babbled on, "She could be a psycho-killer." *Or me.*

His eyebrows raised even more; his look made it clear that I was acting like a crazy person. He laughed. "Em, c'mon. What are you talking about? I— "

A muffled *ringing* interrupted him.

Oh no. Please no.

He glanced at his phone, which lay silent. His searching gaze continued—the floor, a quick check of the back seat, before his scrutiny finally located the source of the sound. Raising his eyes from where they'd landed on my lap, his expression turned to one of amusement.

The ringing continued.

"Uh, Em, I think your butt's ringing." He raised an eyebrow.

"Oh, yeah, I…ah, think you're right."

Giving up, I reached beneath my legs to grab the phone, smiling weakly. I quickly hit answer, and gave a too-cheery "Hello?"

I threw my hand out in the air as if to say, "*What can you do*?"

The voice on the other end of the phone dispelled any embarrassment about being caught hiding a phone in an awkward spot. I pulled the receiver slightly away from my ear to prevent permanent damage from the raised voice coming through the line.

"Emma! Where in the world are you? I got a call from your mother, and she says you're not in class. I want to know what's going on right now. Are you okay?"

I tried to get a word in. "Dad, I'm fine. Just calm down a minute."

Flinching, I shot Eli a look, and mouthed, "*They know*."

Apparently telling my dad to calm down didn't fall under the wisest course of action in the given situation. When a break finally came that allowed me to speak, I attempted to keep my voice apologetic.

"Dad, I'm sorry if I worried you and Mom. We just decided to bag one day. *One.*"

My forehead began to sweat a little. I was no good under fire. "I don't even get how you knew."

"How is how I know important right now, young lady?"

"No, fine, you're right, it doesn't matter. But we were going to be home by like 8:00 or so. It's not like we were taking off for the night."

"Put Eli on the phone right now. I want to speak to him." Dad sounded like he meant business.

I sighed. "Hold on." I held the phone out toward Eli. "He wants to talk to you."

Eli's eyebrows shot halfway up his head, and he motioned *no way*, and then pointed toward the steering wheel.

"Chicken," I mouthed, returning the phone to my ear. "Dad, he can't talk, he's driving." Sigh. "Fine, I'll tell him... *Fine*... Yes, I know... I will. I promise. Okay, love you too. Bye."

I tilted my head and shot Eli an exaggerated fake smile before I announced, "Well, our road trip is now canceled."

I bent over, reached underneath the seat, and tugged hard to free my bag. "We're due home in no more than two hours. And by the way, your parents apparently know, too."

He hung his head and silently looked for a turnaround.

Chapter Eleven

Emma

After a substantial lecture from both my parents after Mom got home from work at 4:00, I'd retreated to my bedroom.

Dad had gotten a call at his home office after I missed an orthodontist appointment. I never kept track of stuff like that, Mom did. She wrote everything on the giant whiteboard calendar in the kitchen. Somehow, Mom forgot to put this one on, so I was clueless to the fact that I was supposed to be at Dr. Solga's office at 9:45.

From there, Dad called Mom at school to make sure everything was okay, and that we hadn't gotten into an accident or something on the way to the appointment. For a grown man, my father could tend to be a bit dramatic. It all completely snowballed after that. Mom called the dentist, who agreed to squeeze me in if I could come over right away. But when I didn't answer the page to report to the Guidance Office so we could leave, Mom sent a note down to my History classroom for the teacher to give to me. I obviously wasn't there to get it.

Upon hearing this, my mother turned into full-out detective mode and apparently questioned a mass of students, finally piecing together that someone saw me crab-walking *(embarrassing!)* to Eli's car earlier that morning, and someone else watched as we left the school parking lot. It didn't take much after that for Mom to discover that Eli wasn't in school either, put two and two together, and figure out we'd both ditched for the day.

Sarah sent me a couple of texts while I was downstairs getting chewed out. Apparently the news of us sneaking out made the school gossip vine, clearly ranking of higher interest to everyone since there was more questioning going on in an effort to solve my absence than in an episode of *Criminal Minds*.

Sighing, I crossed over to the small white futon pushed against my far bedroom wall. Sitting on it was preferable to my bed when I wanted to catch the breeze from my room's front windows.

I dialed Sarah's number as I propped my feet up on an overturned purple milk crate that I used for a table. As the phone rang, I logged in to Facebook. Guess it was time for Kelli to make another status update.

I decided to make it easy and just go with a quote. Eli would probably appreciate intellectual instead of just a breakdown of the day's menu or a not-so-humorous cat meme.

A sudden cheery voice asking me to leave a message startled me. Shoot. I really wanted to talk to Sarah. As I stared dejectedly at the computer screen, I obliged the recorded request. "Hey, it's me. Where are you? We need to talk. Call me as soon as you get this. I think the plan is finally working, but there's a slight hiccup. Call me!"

I absently set the phone down and resumed the task of

figuring out the perfect status update. It had to be one that somehow sent a message. After I googled a few ideas, I found the perfect quote.

Apparently there is nothing that cannot happen today. ~Mark Twain

It fit. Maybe a little obscure, but still. It wasn't anything overly mushy and obvious, but still worked given the situation. Plus, I knew Twain was one of Eli's favorite authors.

The phone rang just as I finished.

Forgoing the normal greeting, I started right in. "I need your help."

"Well, hello to you, too." Sarah had the same calm tone as always, ignoring my hysteria. "So where'd you disappear to today? Your mom was practically leading a search party."

I stood up and walked over to close my bedroom door before answering. "Don't get me started. Eli and I were just planning to drive to the beach for the day and— "

"What?" Her voice went uncharacteristically loud. "Whoa, back up a second. Whose idea was that?"

"How did you not hear about this? I thought everybody knew."

"Well, I didn't. At least not where you were going. And thanks for answering my texts earlier by the way." She cleared her throat loudly to show her displeasure. "I only heard you took off, and didn't sign out or whatever, and your mom was questioning half the school."

I tilted my head back against the wall and moaned, "I can't stand that she works there. Seriously."

"Anyway…" She'd heard me whine about my mom being our school's guidance counselor plenty of times before. "Go back to the part about you two going to the beach together. How did *that* happen?"

Sarah was the only person who knew how I really felt about Eli. All of it. She constantly tried to convince me to,

"*Just tell him already,*" and even offered to have her boyfriend, Doug, talk to Eli, and try to find out if I had a shot. But I didn't want to do that either, so I'd sworn her to secrecy.

"I'm still not even sure how it happened. After English, he was standing outside the classroom window with a sign telling me to meet him."

"Wow, total Cusack move. All he needed was a boombox over his head."

"I know, right? Anyway, I left school— "

"Which I still can't believe you did by the way."

"And we ended up driving for like an hour before he even told me where we were going."

There was a pause before she asked, "So, did you tell him about you being Kelli?"

"Are you kidding me? No! We've only messaged back and forth a few times. It's too soon. But, I've decided against the whole phone call thing."

"Because the computer thing is working so well for you."

A crash carried through the line, followed by loud crying. "Ugh, I have to go. I'm supposed to be watching Scotty while my mom runs to the store. He just broke something again."

"The kid does have a future in MMA."

"Cute."

"Okay, well call me later once you're off babysitting duty."

"I still have a huge Chem test I've got to study for, but if I have time after that I will," she promised.

"All right. Good luck with your brother."

"Ha, thanks." Sounds of wailing in the background continued until the call disconnected.

I should probably get busy with some of my own schoolwork too. There was that paper to finish for Civics, and I needed to start studying for my Spanish test.

I decided to get a drink before I got started. As I walked down the hallway toward the stairs, I stopped abruptly at the sound of my name. I leaned over the railing overlooking the family room below, and almost tipped right over when I heard, "…they're having sex?"

Whoa, *what*?

Tiptoeing to the stairs, I strained to listen. They were too far away. I took the steps one at a time, making sure to skip the second from the top, since it creaked. I bent over as I descended, making every effort to make myself as small as possible in addition to silent. Why hadn't I taken my shoes off?

Voices carried toward me, slightly louder the closer I got to the first floor.

"…not. But we can't be sure. After all, they spend all that time together." That was my dad.

Silence ensued after that comment. I had to hear what exactly they were talking about.

As I neared the bottom, I didn't want to risk being seen, so I remained crouched down on the last step instead of moving onto the open landing. All breathing stopped as I waited for my mother's response.

"Well, it would probably be naive to just ignore the possibility. We have to be realistic about it. I certainly hope they aren't, she's just too young. But, on the other hand, if they are, I want her to know she can come to us."

Mom paused, and I made out the sound of ice in a glass. "Maybe I should talk to her. Or to both of them. Just be straight-forward and bring up the issue of safe sex."

Omigod.

This couldn't be happening. My parents weren't actually sitting in there calmly discussing my sex life. Well, in reality, my non-existent sex life, but still! A shrink father and guidance counselor mom—only kids lucky enough to hit that parental jackpot would have to suffer through this.

Yet how could they think I was having sex? I didn't even date. Sure, Eli and I were together all the time, *but not like that.*

No way would I let my mom sit Eli and me down and ask us if we were having sex. Just the thought of it made me want to crawl in a hole and die of embarrassment.

Thirst forgotten, I scrambled back up the stairs as fast as humanly possible. I needed to call Sarah back and get some advice. Hopefully Scotty went down for a nap or something by now.

I dialed Sarah's number. "C'mon, pick up…please pick up."

But she didn't. At the sound of her voicemail, I hung up in frustration. "Super," I muttered.

I tried desperately to figure out what to do about the new problem at hand. Should I simply confront my parents about what I'd overheard? Just let it go and hope they dropped it? Or move out of the country in the middle of the night and change my name to Ileisha or something equally exotic? It was as if someone had dropped me in the middle of some bad after-school special.

Since no answers flashed from the heavens, I decided that I might as well try to get some homework done before I drove myself crazy. I wanted to forget all about it for a while, so I got up and crossed over to my desk, and realized I didn't even have all of the books I needed from school, since I hadn't bothered to grab them when Eli and I took off earlier. Fabulous.

Oh well, it gave me an excuse to check Kelli's page. Like I really needed one. The screen displayed a new message from Eli. I eagerly clicked it open.

> *You really surprised me with that quote. What made you pick that one? I always like using ones I can somehow relate to. Or even song lyrics. Like this one … "I feel like you know me. Well, I've tried to let you see me for yourself. I feel like I'm…I'm out of my head; I've got this thing for you." :) E.*

Holy crap. What he wrote was the next best thing to

coming right out and saying he really liked me.

No, it was the next best thing to coming out and saying he really liked Kelli, the little voice in my head reminded me. I told the voice to shut up.

Maybe this whole thing was stupid. I mean, if he really fell for Kelli, he was going to be so pissed when he realized I'd set it up and lied to him. The realization of how badly I was betraying his trust and friendship started to gnaw at my gut. There was nothing I could do about it now but keep it up. And believe he'd understand when the time came. I closed my eyes a second, still slightly nauseous.

Okay, I had to say something back to him, something to let him know I felt the same. It had to be short—I couldn't reveal too much yet. I thought for a minute, then slowly typed out, *There are so many things I wish I could say to you.*

Well that was true enough.

I hoped to see a return message right away, so I sat still, staring at the inbox. I had to keep reminding myself to stop holding my breath. I watched, and waited. And waited some more. Finally, a new message appeared.

> *So just tell me the things you'd like to say. I'm listening. I'd REALLY like you to. :)*

Yeah, right. He made it sound so simple when it was anything but. Wiggling my bare toes under my chair, I finally answered,

> *It's not that easy. And you don't even know me. Not really.*

An instant message popped up. I'd almost been expecting it this time.

> *So tell me about you. The real you. Not the you that you show to people online.*

I wanted to. I really did. It would be amazing to talk with my own real thoughts, even if I had to type them as Kelli. But what to say?

The past couple of years, I'd gotten used to hiding pieces of myself even from him, because I was scared. I was deathly afraid that he'd be able to see through the masks I wore sometimes to keep from letting him see how much I really liked him. That it was so much more than friendship.

He inspired me, challenged me, and made me feel good about myself. He made all the stupid, trivial things going on at different times in my life seem unimportant. I knew he believed in me, and that helped me to believe in myself more too.

How was I supposed to say all of that to a guy I'd supposedly just met?

Instead, I settled for,

I can just tell you're the kind of guy who inspires the people around him. Me? I'm not always sure of different things in my life, and I just really think that's an amazing quality to have. You know?

The screen showed he was typing a reply. It appeared a moment later.

Yeah, I do. But I'd be willing to bet you inspire more people than you realize. I'll leave it at that. I have to go, but know this, from different things you've said, I'm pretty sure I can see the real you. And you have no reason to be unsure of anything. Talk Soon, E.

And he was gone, just like that.

"Argh!" Dropping my head in my hands, not for the first time I wished that I were more skilled at the whole guy/girl thing and better at reading him.

Yet, another part of me felt upset about how easily he

seemed to relate and respond to fictional Kelli. It didn't seem to bother him in the least to be romantically chatting it up and sending lines from songs to some girl he just met. Why couldn't he have done that for me? Why didn't I inspire poetry and songs?

Emotionally drained, I rested my head on the desk, not wanting to think about it anymore. It was too depressing. I must have dozed off, because the next thing I knew, Mom called to me from the bottom of the stairs.

"Emma, time for dinner!"

I lifted my head just enough to check the time, and saw it was already 6:30. Wow. I must have been out for over an hour. That explained the stiff neck and damp spot along my cheek; I must have been drooling in my sleep.

"Okay, be right there!" I pulled myself up from my semi-prone position like an eighty-year-old woman facing the firing squad.

Please don't let them actually decide to have a sex chat with me over dinner. And if that *was* the plan, I prayed God would take pity on me and send a lightning bolt my way. Before the salad course would be nice.

As I trudged downstairs, I decided that they'd probably be even more embarrassed than I was about the entire topic, and wouldn't bring it up. Plus, they had to know there was nothing to worry about, anyway.

Feeling marginally better, as I walked into our large eat-in kitchen I called out, "Do you need any help, Mom?"

"No thanks, honey. We're in here."

In here? In where? It sounded like Mom's voice came from the dining room, only we never ate in there. Well, except for holidays when my Aunt Karen and Uncle Matt came to visit with their kids.

I crossed to the old-fashioned French doors that led to the formal dining room. As they swung open, I understood the formality.

Because seated at the table was my mother, an empty chair next to her. Across the table sat my father, who looked meticulous as usual in his button-down dress shirt, even with the top button undone. And seated to Dad's right, looking utterly cute in a loose, white polo shirt, was Eli.

What was he doing here? I immediately moved my hand to my hair, remembering what I must look like after my little nap. Then a horrible feeling rushed through me. Wait…oh no. Let this please just be a casual, impromptu dinner.

The feeling of dread refused to go away. I'd learned to trust my instincts when it came to my parents and their ability to publically humiliate me.

"Honey, sit. Here, there's a seat right next to me." Mom motioned me toward the empty chair at the table.

Finally drawing the courage to look directly at Eli for the first time since I entered the room, I tried to read his expression.

He offered me a small, bewildered smile, along with his *What the heck's going on* face.

I smiled back half-heartedly and hesitantly slipped into the empty seat.

Just as I took a sip of water from the glass next to my plate, my mother cleared her throat, as though preparing for a speaking engagement.

After a dainty tip of her head toward each of us in turn, she announced, "I thought it may be fitting to bring the four of us together."

I choked on my water. Oh dear Lord in heaven. No. *Please no.*

Eli now looked completely bewildered. I'm sure he was wondering what the heck he'd been invited to.

"Now, Rob and I just want you both to know that we love you both very much." Mom motioned toward Eli and me with that one.

Eli shot me the *what the heck* look again. Twice in two minutes didn't bode well.

There were no words. I shook my head before fixating on the empty white dinner plate with the gold leaf etchings resting on the table in front of me.

Mom talked on, although her voice sounded a little forced, like she was trying too hard to be diplomatic. I guess there was some difficulty in trying to play the counselor when you also happened to be the parent.

"As you are both getting to be of a certain age, you'll be curious about some things. You may even feel as though you want to experience different things."

She sounded like she was giving some formal speech. I pressed my eyes closed so tightly for several seconds that I saw little white squiggles.

She took a breath, but then Dad jumped in with, "Now, we understand that these feelings and urges are completely normal at your age." Like Mom, he sounded so professional, even though his neck was slightly purple under his collar.

Oh. My. God. This was really happening. They were seriously doing it, having a sex talk with me and Eli, together. I wouldn't have been able to look at him if you paid me a million dollars. My cheeks had to be the color of ripe, summer tomatoes.

Mom must have started back up while I zoned out praying this was some type of lucid dream, because when I finally started listening again, she was mid-roll in full guidance counselor mode.

"...just want to make sure you are familiar with the terms STDs, condoms, and unplanned pregnancy."

Okay, that was enough. I couldn't sit here and listen to a Sex-Ed talk given by my parents while Eli sat across the table from me. Why couldn't I have normal parents who didn't even want to say the "S" word in front of their kids?

I stood up, face on fire, and spun away from the table. I fought to keep my tears at bay. "I'm done. This is too much, even for you two."

As I started to walk away, a noise came from across the wide cherry wood table. A rumbling sound that within seconds burst into full-scale roaring laughter.

When I turned to look back, Eli held his hands over his mouth, as if he could shove the laugh back in. Our eyes caught, and I finally lost it as well. Mad giggles poured out of me, and then turned into flat out hiccups from trying to gulp down the hysteria. Tears rolled down my cheeks.

My parents both sat back in their seats, two sets of eyes moving from me to Eli and back again, clearly not understanding what was so funny.

Eli stood as well. "I'm going to be heading home, but thanks so much for the ..." He couldn't finish the sentence, so he instead chose to wave his goodbyes as he continued fighting back a grin. As he passed me, he reached out and squeezed my hand.

I smiled, appreciating the gesture.

Unreal. I shook my head after the front door closed and headed toward the stairs to escape to my room. After that show, I didn't really have an appetite anymore.

Once again, Eli had saved the day. He'd turned my complete mortification into something I could actually smile about.

After my shower, as I stood in a robe combing out my damp hair in front of the bathroom mirror, I shook my head and grinned.

He really was something. No doubt about it.

And more than ever, I wanted that "something" to become "boyfriend."

Chapter Twelve

Emma

"You've got to be kidding me." Sarah shoveled a mass of limp green lettuce leaves into her mouth, and chewed furiously. Her dark glasses bounced slightly on the bridge of her nose with each chew.

"I wish I were." As I absently moved the day's cafeteria mystery meat around my plate with a plastic fork, I shook my head.

Bess and Shaina sat with us at the school lunch table, too engrossed as they giggled over muted racy YouTube videos on Shaina's phone to pay much attention to our conversation going on across the table. Shaina pointed to the phone's screen and covered her mouth, blushing.

Sarah glanced their way and rolled her eyes. "It's like we're back in middle school, I swear."

"Seriously, you have to help me." I grimaced. "I hid in the bathroom between any classes where I knew I'd see him today. I feel like an idiot, and have no idea what I'm supposed to say to him after my parents pulled that stunt last night."

Sarah moved on from what the cafeteria menu generously described as a "fresh garden salad" to slightly safer territory, canned fruit cocktail. Who said school lunch programs were sub-par?

She shrugged as she stirred the squared fruit in the tiny speckled cup. "I wouldn't worry too much about it. I mean, you said he was cool with the whole thing. That he laughed it off."

I finally gave up on any attempts to consume the congealed brown mess in front of me, and pushed the tray away before I nervously twisted a stray curl around my finger.

"Well yeah, but what else was he gonna do?" I drummed my fingernails on the table. "And besides, now he *has* to think there's a reason my parents would even say something like that. What if he thinks I told my parents I like him?" I shook my head in frustration. "This could ruin everything."

"Uh, no. This could help everything. I'm sorry, but I seriously think your little catfish scheme is going to blow up in your face if you don't stop it now."

Bess briefly looked up from the *How to put a condom on a banana* video tutorial she was watching. "Oh, I love that show. Those people are whacked."

"Anyway"—I rolled my eyes—"I think I'm going to—"

A quick kick to my shin under the table made me break off sharing my latest plan. "Ow! What the heck?"

Sarah jerked her chin to the right, eyes widened in unspoken warning.

"Please tell me he isn't coming this way," I whispered as I watched Sarah's eyes follow someone behind me.

"Hey! How's it going?" Sarah asked with a staged expression of surprise.

Crap. I forced a smile and willed the flush creeping above my white tailored collar to disappear. I slowly turned to face the person I'd been trying so hard to avoid all morning.

Eli walked the remaining few steps to where I sat on the long bench. His well-worn jeans were low-slung on his hips, and showed off his strong thigh muscles to perfection. The black fitted T-shirt he wore managed to be casual-preppy and sexy all at once. There was no sign of the dimple I loved so much, given the perplexed frown on his face.

He stopped directly in front of me, so I found myself eye-level with his well-defined abs. Normally not a view to complain about, I couldn't help but avert my gaze as I remembered the topic of last night's humiliation.

When I didn't meet his eyes, he swung a leg over the bench and straddled it. "Where were you this morning? I kept looking for you, but it seemed like you were avoiding me."

Sarah jumped up. "Well, I need to go to the library to get something. I'll see you guys later." She grabbed her lunch tray as she stood before walking away with a little wave.

"Gee, that was subtle," I muttered.

Eli sat still, waiting.

Not sure what to say, I resumed playing with the mystery meat on my plate, head down. Hair spilled over my shoulders, half covering my face, as I studiously tried to avoid his questioning look.

He reached out and tentatively touched a loose curl. "I really like your hair down, You should wear it this way more often."

I sat frozen, the hand holding my fork halted mid-pattern in the gelatinous brown sauce. Like the game freeze tag we played as kids, I couldn't move after he touched me.

I self-consciously cleared my throat. "I'm sorry. You're right. I guess I was sort of avoiding you."

He uncharacteristically ran his hand down through my hair until it rested on the top of my shoulder. "Why?" His voice was quiet.

I jerked my head up to face him. "*Why*? Because my

parents acted like crazy people last night."

Laugh lines crinkled around his eyes as he smiled. "So? Everybody's parents make an art form of embarrassing their kids at one point or another." He shifted a little closer to me. "And after all, it's not like we haven't bra shopped together," he teased.

I gave in, and laughed. "Oh, you wish!"

He tilted his head a little to the side, his teeth grabbing his full lower lip. "You think?"

My cheeks burned under his intense scrutiny. I cleared my throat again.

A slow smile spread across his face, his expression one of satisfaction mixed with curiosity.

The warning bell rang, a signal that students had only two minutes to finish their lunches and return all trays before heading to their lockers.

Spell broken, I inched away from him and stood. He reached out for my tray as I began to lift it off the table.

"Allow me."

Before I could utter a word in protest, he stood next to me, and grabbed my tray to deposit in one of the giant plastic bins filling the counters against the cafeteria wall.

As he walked away, tray in hand, he turned his head and winked directly at me, mouthing the words, "*We'll talk later.*"

Oh boy.

Mr. Jones decided to throw a pop quiz our way in Science. I usually aced his class, but my mind kept wandering to how Eli acted at lunch. It once again seemed like he'd almost been flirting, which made no sense.

I tapped the eraser of my pencil on my overturned paper as I waited for the teacher to call time on the quiz so we could correct them.

Eli had winked at me. And played with my hair. I imagined him leaning in, breath warm on my face as he leaned in closer, closer…

A sharp poke in the center of my back shook me from the delicious daydream. Warmth filled my cheeks as I realized Mr. Jones was staring directly at me. Apparently, it wasn't the first time he'd called my name.

"Emma, what is the answer for the second question?" His look was stern.

I flipped my paper over, embarrassed to be caught not paying attention. "Umm…os… osmosis."

"Correct. Daniel, question three?"

I sighed, and sank down slightly in my chair.

"Loser." The whispered hiss came from the seat next to me. Carissa smirked, obviously thrilled that I'd landed on the teacher's radar.

She really needed to come up with a new insult. I turned my head to face forward again, but she wasn't used to being ignored. She whispered, "I saw you talking to Eli earlier." I shot her a quick glance. Her eyes narrowed, and she looked me up and down pointedly.

My jaw set. What the hell did she care who I talked to?

"Don't you think it's kind of pathetic how you keep following him around like a puppy dog? Seriously, like he'd ever go for someone like you."

I clenched my teeth, refusing to allow her to see how much the words stung.

"Okay, class. Please pass your papers forward. Be sure to write the number of correct answers at the top of your page, and circle the number." Mr. Jones walked to the first row to begin collecting our quizzes.

Perfect. I hadn't been paying attention thanks to Carissa, and had missed more than half of the ten answers. When I received the stack of quizzes, I tried to hurry and check the answers of the students from behind me against my own.

Chuck, the tall kid who sat in front of me, rolled his eyes impatiently as I marked my quiz in record time. "Sorry. Here." I handed him the stack after I'd finished. I'd gotten five wrong. My grades were definitely starting to drop over the past week or so. Too much time spent worrying about the whole Eli/ Kelli thing.

School was important to me, always had been, but lately I'd been distracted. I'd always made fun of girls like that, ones who put boys ahead of anything else. I wasn't proud that I was turning into one.

When class ended, I stood up to head to my locker. As I walked through the door, Carissa shoved by to bounce over to where Chase, her flavor of the week boy toy, waited across the hall.

She stood on tiptoe to offer him a kiss. He willingly obliged, then slung his big, beefy arm around her tiny shoulders. She giggled and ran her hand across his chest. Chase stared down at her like she was a princess in some story.

I shuffled past them, feeling sick. Why was it so easy for some girls? They always seemed to know just what to say, how to act, how to get a guy's attention. The thought of Carissa resorting to something as pathetic as creating a fake profile to get a guy to notice her was ludicrous. Most girls I knew seemed to have some inherent ability to flirt; I didn't possess that gene.

Despite Eli's promise at lunch that we would talk later, I hadn't seen him the rest of the day. I wanted to text him, but I'd forgotten to charge my phone last night, and the battery had died fifth period.

I sighed as I closed my locker. Happy couples surrounded me—they laughed and stole kisses as they walked down the hall to head out, fingers laced together. I turned and walked out of school alone.

Chapter Thirteen

Eli

I scanned the student parking area for Emma after the last bell. I'd tried to text her twice, asking if I could give her a ride home, but she'd never answered. I had no idea what was up, or why she was ignoring me.

At lunch today, there'd been some real chemistry between us. The look I'd seen in her eyes…I couldn't have imagined it. I banged my head back against the headrest. To think all these years I'd been such a freaking idiot.

Hopefully I'd be able to catch her, and we could talk. I leaned forward and turned the radio on, needing the music.

"Yo, Perry! Paintball this weekend, you coming?" Corey Roberts made trigger motions with his hand as he climbed in his truck parked a few spaces over.

"Sure. Who all's gonna be there?"

"So far we've got you, me, Raider, Tony, Doug, and a few others." He slammed his door. "I'm gonna kick your ass!" He laughed.

"Keep dreaming." I waved as he pulled out, and then scanned the lot again. I couldn't see her bus, so I must have missed her, or she caught a ride with Sarah. *Shit.*

Long brown curls over by the bus landing caught my attention. Gorgeous, familiar curls. I quickly started the car.

A crew of cheerleaders briefly blocked her from my view as I pulled up to the curb. I rolled my eyes as Carissa offered a flirty wave. I couldn't believe I'd once had a thing for her. Light years ago. Then again, back then she wasn't such a bitch.

I honked the horn, hoping to attract Emma's attention, but she didn't look over, so I rolled down the passenger side window and called out, "Em! Hey, Emma!"

Her head popped up, and when our eyes met her eyes brightened. The sight of her did weird things to my gut, things I wasn't used to, but in a really good way. A grin took over my face as I waved. When she walked towards me, I leaned over to open the door. As she stepped in the car, I couldn't stop my eyes from following the path of her legs. I swallowed hard, and told myself to stop being such a dog.

I looked up to see if she'd caught me, but she was smiling, no idea I'd been imagining all kinds of things that I had no right to imagine involving her legs being wrapped around me. I smiled back, hoping it came across normal, not lecherous. I sucked. I was officially turning into Kevin.

"Thanks." She looked for space to set her stuff.

"Oh, sorry." I grabbed a fast food bag and a couple of empty water bottles from the front seat and shoved them in the back. I cleared my throat a little self-consciously before gunning the motor and pulling out.

"No problem." She poked my leg. "So, I had this quiz in Chemistry, bombed again."

"That sucks."

"I know, right?"

When she adjusted her seatbelt, it drew my attention to

the open buttons on the neckline of her shirt. I couldn't tear my eyes away. It was as if I was looking at Emma through a brand new lens, and I couldn't get enough of her. I wanted to drink in every detail. The curve of her cheek, the way her collar fell against her neck, the…

"Are you listening?" She stared at me, eyebrows drawn together. I realized I'd missed whatever she'd been saying the past minute or so.

I raised my eyes, mortified. "What? Oh, yeah. Sorry. I thought I saw something on your shirt. I didn't know if there was a bug on you." *A bug?*

"Ew! Where? Get it off!" She slapped and swiped at the non-existent bug.

"I think you got it, you're good. Um, sorry, what were you saying?"

"Never mind, I was just babbling about the quiz. Not important. So…you wanted to talk?" She bit her lip and glanced at me from half lowered lashes.

I swallowed, not sure how to bring up what I really wanted to talk about. The whole Facebook thing. I wanted us to just stop dancing around and playing games. I liked her. I hoped she liked me. I wanted us to try to take it to the next level, to see what could happen.

I sucked in a deep breath for courage.

"Right. So." I met her gaze for a second before looking back at the road. "I felt kind of weird at first bringing this up, but then again, we aren't kids anymore, and we both know the score, and by now you know how I feel, so…" I glanced over again.

She didn't say anything, just picked at a piece of lint on her skirt. Was I supposed to spell it out? This was so awkward. I rubbed the back of my neck.

"I'll just ask you." Maybe she wasn't interested. If that was the case, I was saying all of this and looking like an ass. Maybe she did the whole profile thing as a goof to mess around. But I had to know, either way.

Now or never. I drew in another long breath before blurting out. "So what do you think?"

She just stared at me. Not saying a word.

Well, shit.

Chapter Fourteen

Emma

Eli's head bent toward me in a half-nod, and he looked way more nervous than I'd ever seen him before.

That was it?

What did I think?

How was I supposed to respond to that? Was I supposed to know what he was talking about? A sinking feeling of dread came over me. *Did he know?*

I stared at him, trying to read his expression. He didn't look mad, so he probably didn't know about the profile, but I'd seem stupid asking for clarification since he seemed to think we were on the same page. I wasn't even sure we were reading the same book.

Talk about frustrating. Things didn't used to be this difficult between us. Before, we both knew what the other was thinking without saying a word. But ever since the whole Facebook debacle, I was constantly on guard, second-guessing his every word or action.

I tried to play it cool, not lost in the least, and gave him a hesitant smile and nodded. "Um…yeah, okay." Agreeing with him was the safest course of action. Although I could be raving about mad scientists creating killer babies for all I knew.

But considering the way he'd been behaving lately, a part of me wondered if there could actually be a chance he was into me too. Was he talking about *us*? Like, as in a couple *us*? It seemed too much to hope for. I wished he'd spill whatever he was trying to say, so I didn't have to try to fill in the blanks, but I was too afraid to ask him what the hell he was jabbering about. The lion in Oz had more courage than me.

He broke into a grin. "Really? Great! I was so freaked at first, thinking I was reading you wrong or something." He watched me expectantly.

A smile burst across my face. This was it—it had to be. I wanted to reach out, grab him and scream, *finally*!

Eli's matching smile grew even wider. "That's a relief. I mean, I wasn't sure if you thought it was a good idea, too. I mean, or if you thought it was just a joke or what. But then, I kind of had a feeling, or hoped anyway. And when I brought it up the other day…"

He broke off when a car backed out in front of us, and he reached his hand out in front of me reflexively. "Sorry about that."

I shook my head. "Um…no problem." Lost in my thoughts, I hadn't even noticed our near miss. I was completely confused now. He hadn't brought up anything about us before.

He slowed down and pulled into his driveway, stopped the car, and turned to face me directly. He reached down and rested his hand lightly on my leg.

I'd just decided to go for broke and ask him what exactly he was talking about when he continued on, stopping my questions.

His voice turned more serious, "The other day when we were talking about Kelli, and I told you I wanted to ask her out, I—"

"Oh!" I clapped my hand over my mouth. Mortified, I realized I *had* gotten it wrong, misinterpreted his signals. I'd been seeing what I wanted to see, not what was really there.

Waves of jealousy over a fictional girl that I'd created consumed me. Welcome to a new low, ladies and gentleman. But I put on a brave face.

"Of course. I totally think you should ask her out. After all, why not, right? You aren't seeing anybody else, or…"

"Em, wait." His eyes scrunched up as he watched my lips move.

"What? No, I completely agree. I should have never said anything against it before. She sounds great." I nodded my head like a bobble-toy. "And she's obviously the type of girl you're looking for. Beautiful and all."

My teeth bared in what I hoped passed for an encouraging smile, and not a nauseous grimace. I prayed I wouldn't puke in his car. "Hey I have an idea! This'll be fun, maybe we can double."

What the hell was I saying?

Eli pulled back, and shook his head slowly. "I thought, I guess I thought…" His voice staggered off.

"I know, at first I probably seemed kind of against the idea. After all, I was worried about how well you really knew this girl, but, hey, you like her, right? That's all that matters. And I'm sure she's really into you."

Inane word vomit spewed out of my mouth, but I was helpless to stop it. I smiled brightly, trying to cover the rush of pain inside. I refused to let it show. How could I have thought for even one minute that he'd been talking about me? That he actually felt that way about me. And why did it bother me so much when this was my plan all along?

He ran his fingers through his wind-blown hair, still shaking his head. He looked down at his hands where they now rested on the steering wheel. After a heartbeat that lasted forever, he lifted his head and met my eyes once more. "So, let me get this straight. You're saying you want me to ask Kelli out, and you want to go on a *double date* with us?"

I nodded, trying not to show how sick I felt inside.

What the hell am I saying? How am I going to get out of this now? Word vomit. I blamed it all on the word vomit I was so famous for when nervous.

"Well, sure. Or do think that would be weird?"

"Uh, actually, yeah."

"Why?" I looked at him sharply.

He only stared back.

Suddenly offended, it hit that apparently I hadn't hidden my feelings as well as I thought. He *did* know I liked him, and just assumed I'd act like a five year old and stomp and pitch a fit if I was around him and another girl. Clearly that was what he'd meant with his whole "We're not kids and we both know the score" speech.

So what was with all of his flirty little comments at the lunch table earlier, or the other night? Practicing out his moves so he could have them all down pat to use on the girl he *really* liked?

I wanted to jump out of the car before he could see how humiliated I felt. Hurt built into anger. He must have loved watching me blush and fawn over him. Carissa was right. I needed to get out of the car, get to my room, and bawl my eyes out in private.

Pride crushed, it was best to go on the offensive, convince him he had it all wrong. It was clear *his* interest lay in a certain blond cheerleader, and not with me.

And even though a part of me screamed, "*Well that was The Plan,*" another part of me broke inside, because I'd allowed myself to believe that maybe he'd finally seen me, *really* seen me, and wanted to be with me, *the real me*, not the one hiding behind a fake photo.

I'd made the mistake of allowing myself to hope, and now his words crushed that hope to dust. I still wasn't good enough.

I shot him a withering look, and turned my voice saccharine sweet. "I think I can handle it. After all, I'll be busy with my own date, remember?" The cotton candy smile was all for show, my eyes shot sparks.

Eli gasped like he'd been sucker-punched. Then his eyes darkened. "Fine," he bit out. "I was obviously wrong. I won't make that mistake again."

"Fine," I echoed.

"Fine!"

Clueless as to what *he* had to be angry about, I just wanted out. Seething, I pushed open the passenger side door with more force than necessary and watched in horror as it slammed directly into the tall pole attached to a basketball hoop set up at the edge of Eli's driveway. Metal crashing against metal reverberated through the early afternoon air.

He jumped out, staring. "Oh, well that's just great. Way to go."

My eyes widened in disbelief as I pointed at the pole. "And this is my fault, how?"

"I'm not the one that smashed the door into it."

"*I'm* not the one who parked the car too close."

"Well, you could have looked at what you were doing."

"Well, *you* could have looked at where you were parking!"

He stared at me in stony silence.

I crossed my arms and yelled, "I opened my damn door, Eli! That's all. So unless you wanted me to levitate out of the car, this wasn't my fault!"

He stood near the passenger side bumper. Tension seeped out of every pore. "Fine, whatever. After all, what do

I know?" He seemed hurt and bitter and for the life of me, I couldn't figure out why. "Maybe your new *boyfriend* can give you a ride home from school from now on."

"Fine! And maybe you can cart Kelli's skinny little ass anywhere she needs to go," I shot back.

"Maybe I will! And I bet she knows how to open a damn door!" With that, he spun away and stalked up the front steps to his house. He didn't look back once.

After slamming the passenger door closed, I crossed the yard to my own home. Sick to the stomach, I couldn't figure out how the day had gone from Eli whispering how he liked my hair, to him yelling at me about something that wasn't even my fault and stomping away.

And the craziest part was that thanks to my latest brilliant suggestion, I only had a few days to find myself a fake boyfriend, and even worse, find a girl to play Eli's new online girlfriend so we could all go on some ridiculous double date.

Covering my face with my hands, I whispered, "Things *cannot* get any worse."

Until they did.

Chapter Fifteen

Emma

"And he hasn't talked to me once this entire week since then," I muttered as I reached out to grab a book from the bottom shelf without bothering to glance at the title.

I'd invaded Buy the Book about forty minutes earlier, two hours before Sarah's shift in the small bookstore was scheduled to end, but I couldn't wait that long to talk to her. Instead, I trailed behind as Sarah checked inventory in the Women's Fiction and Young Adult sections, plopping down in the middle of whatever aisle she was currently cataloguing. Buy the Book hadn't yet progressed to the computer age.

She reached down and snatched a paperback out of my hands. "Emma, all you're doing is messing up the shelves and making more work for me. Please stop."

After placing the book back in the correct spot on the low shelf, she straightened up and lifted her hands to adjust the colorful scarf she wore as a headband. The deep jewel tones of the band complemented her smooth mocha skin and vivid green eyes.

Shaking her head, Sarah dropped down so she was eye-level with me, where I sat on the floor. She reached out an arm, silver bangles tinkling, and grasped my hand as she continued on softer, "Emma, this whole thing was a bad idea. I know you don't want to hear it, and I'm not saying it to be a jerk. But, you had to know it wasn't going to end well."

I lowered my head and fought back tears. "I thought it would work. I thought it would make him realize that deep down he loved me."

"Oh, Em." Sighing, she reached out both arms.

I fell into her comforting embrace, unable to prevent the sobs that burst out. "I hate this, it just hurts so much." I hiccupped through the tears. "I miss him so damn much, and I don't even know what to say to him as Kelli anymore either."

My hands came away smeared with mascara after I wiped my tears. "He emailed her twice this week. I messaged back saying she was sick and wouldn't be online much just so I didn't have to figure out what to say if he really *does* ask her out."

We leaned back against the wooden bookshelves together, neither of us saying a word for a few minutes, Sarah's arm wrapped tight around my shoulder, offering silent support. Thankfully, only one other person was in the store, some college student with a nose ring who ran the register up front. And she was too busy cracking her gum and texting to pay any real attention to us.

I looked up and quietly asked, "What do I do now?"

Sarah shook her head. "I don't know."

We resumed staring at our feet, Sarah's tall leather boots, and my sensible flats.

Curling a leg beneath her, she finally raised her head, a determined gleam in her eyes. "Okay, let's look at this logically. You want to work things out with Eli." She tilted her head, giving me an expectant look.

"Well, obviously."

"Okay, so, how do we make that happen?"

"I don't know! That's the problem!" I wailed.

She held up a hand, halting me. "And every problem has a solution. You just need to solve it, right?"

The urge to roll my eyes was overwhelming, but I knew she was only trying to help. That fact alone made me mutter a half-hearted, "I guess."

"Right now, the way things stand, I think he's upset about the fact that you were rubbing it in his face about going out with this other guy."

I barked out a laugh. "Yeah, right. I'm pretty sure he couldn't care less if I *am* dating some other guy."

Sarah shook her head again. "Emma, I swear, you can be so obtuse sometimes. Look, Eli's had you right there for him every day from the time we were in what, second grade?"

"First," I correctly softly.

"Fine, first grade. The point is, he's used to you always being there. And he's also used to knowing there was no other guy in competition for his place in your life." She bit her lower lip, concentrating. "But now all of a sudden, you're bringing some strange guy into the mix. That's bound to be threatening for him."

"Oh please," I scoffed. "You're making this sound all big and dramatic."

Sarah raised an eyebrow. "*I'm* not the one making it anything. That's all on you two. The last time I saw this much drama, Stephan and Damian were competing for one Elena Gilbert."

I couldn't help but laugh.

"But seriously. If you really want him, and neither of you are willing to come right out and admit that to each other, then it's time to pull out all the stops."

"I did."

Ignoring me, Sarah nodded.

"What are you talking about? What stops?"

"Your new boyfriend will make Eli stop sitting on his ass and taking you for granted. It will force him to admit how he really feels."

Eyes widening, I burst out, "Are you nuts? There's some major flaws in that plan. Let's see"—I ticked them off on my fingers—"One, he isn't even interested in me like that. He made that abundantly clear." Pointing to the next finger I said, "Two, he wants Kelli. *Kelli,*" I repeated, "Not me. And the biggest problem with your brilliant idea"—I waved all ten fingers wildly—"I don't have a new boyfriend! Or anything even remotely close to one." Rant over, I buried my face in my hands.

Sarah allowed the pity-party for all of three seconds before smacking me none too gently on the leg. "Just a minor detail. Because"—she stretched out the word—"I know just where we can find the perfect guy to play your Mr. Right. Or at least your Mr. Pretend to be Right."

My insane friend beamed. "Trust me."

Famous last words.

Chapter Sixteen

Eli

She wanted me to go out on a date with Kelli. *She wanted me to go out on a date with Kelli?* It made absolutely no sense. I'd been so sure Kelli was Emma. Or Emma was Kelli. Or… whatever. I slammed the lid down on my laptop and stood up, pacing my room.

On top of that, I'd sent, whoever it was, two more messages. They'd gone unanswered. Or basically unanswered since I'd gotten the blow-off. Just freaking perfect. Both Emma *and* Kelli now wanted nothing to do with me. I was batting a thousand. I kicked my desk chair, sending it flying across the room.

"Eli, is everything okay?" My mom walked in the room. Great. Caught acting like a two year old throwing a tantrum.

"Yup, everything's fine."

She glanced over at the chair.

"Sorry about that. I was, uh, checking my fantasy football scores and they went down." The lie made zero sense, but it just popped out. The fantasy draft hadn't even started... wouldn't for months. But thankfully Mom was clueless when it came to anything related to a ball. I sighed. Spectacular. Now in addition to a loser, I'd become a liar.

"Well, don't take those things so seriously. They're meant to be fun." She smiled. "Are you going to be here for dinner or do you have plans?"

I'd been hoping to do something with Em after playing paintball with the guys, but clearly that wouldn't be happening. I rotated my shoulders, trying to work out some tension.

"I'll probably grab something after we hit the range. Don't worry about me, but thanks."

She nodded. "Okay, well, have fun. Don't be out too late."

"I won't."

After she left, I sank down on my bed and stared at the ceiling. Normally, I'd talk to Emma if I had a problem, but that option was obviously off the table. I sighed. Maybe Kevin would have some advice. I'd ask him tonight. It was better than nothing.

Chapter Seventeen

Emma

"Oh my God, you're on crack."

Sarah shot me a withering look. "Look, do you want to get Eli once and for all or not?"

"Well, yeah, but not like this." I shook my head as I stared at the strange guy sitting on a basketball in front of me in Sarah's driveway. "I mean, no offense," I added belatedly.

He tipped his head my way. "None taken."

I turned back to the instigator of this brilliant plan. "You seriously don't think this whole idea is just a bit over the top? I've gotten into enough of a hot mess by lying and making stuff up. This?" I ran my hand through my hair, pushing the bangs off my forehead, feeling weary. "This just seems…I don't know. Too much."

"Emma." Sarah adopted a drill-sergeant tone. "Either you admit the truth to him, *all of it*, or"—she motioned to basketball guy—"you need a boyfriend. Stat." Shrugging, she added, "Really, what's the big deal? Jake is here for two weeks with Tony for spring break. He's going back to college after that, so it's completely believable if you two break up then."

I stared at her, not quite able to fathom how things had gotten so out of control that we were even having this conversation. "And how's your brother going to feel about his friend lying and pretending to go out with me?" I finally asked.

She snorted. "Why would Tony care? Jake's a big boy, he can make his own decisions." Sarah brushed away my concerns. "And besides, if you have to have a fake boyfriend, Jake's not half bad."

"Umm…hello? Still right here, you know." Jake waved his hand in the air.

"Shh, we're trying to work this out." Sarah brushed him off without looking his way.

Jake stood, picked up the basketball, and began to dribble it absently. The ball made a hollow *thunking* sound each time it hit the ground. His tall, lanky frame made it obvious why he preferred the sport.

I had to admit, he wasn't bad looking, but her idea was crazy. And to try to pull off that he was suddenly my boyfriend? It'd never work.

"And how are we going to convince Eli that we're dating? I don't even know him." I motioned vaguely in Jake's direction, looking at Sarah the whole time. I felt stupid even having the conversation in front of a guy I'd just met. *About* a guy I'd just met.

Jake stopped bouncing the ball and looked up, slate blue eyes boring into me. "Look, do you really like this guy?"

I nodded, unable to say a word.

"Then why don't you just tell him that?" Rotating the ball back and forth between his large hands in front of his chest, he continued. "This whole thing doesn't make a whole lot of sense to me."

Sarah reached over and knocked the basketball from his grasp. "Jake, you're not helping. Are you in or out?"

He threw his hands up in surrender. "Fine, if she's in, I'll do it. I need someone to hang with nights Tony has to work anyway. It's not like I have anything better to do." Jake looked my way. "No offense."

I rolled my eyes. "None taken."

He winked, then shook his head. "But, I still don't see why you can't tell him." As he turned and walked up the driveway toward the house, he called back over his shoulder, "Let me know where to meet you for our first date, honey." He laughed good-naturedly before heading in the front door.

Embarrassing didn't begin to cut it. I couldn't really be so pathetic that I was enlisting the help of Tony's college roommate to convince Eli that he was in love with me, and just didn't know it yet.

I sighed. "This is nuts, Sarah."

"No, it's perfect. Jake's a nice guy. Like I told you, he's been here before a few times on weekends. It's not like he's some creepo stranger you have to worry about."

We glanced up as a squealing voice carried out the front window. "But I want cookies!"

Sarah shook her head. "Want a younger brother?"

I laughed. "No thanks."

"Anyway, Jake's pretty smart, so it's not like you won't be able to talk to him." She walked over and set the basketball in a large blue storage container filled with sports equipment. "He'll be perfect."

"And what about the fact that there is no Kelli? It's not like Jake and I can really go on a double date with her and Eli."

Sarah thought for a moment. "What about coming up with a reason they can't talk anymore? Now that you have Jake, I think that'll get his attention anyway, so you won't need

Kelli anymore." She added, "Just don't make it right away, or that might look too obvious." She checked her watch. "Look, my mom's at work so I have to go in and start dinner before Scotty convinces Jake to let him eat all of the Oreos. What do you want me to tell him? "

I had a bad feeling about the whole plan, like it was going to blow up in my face. But desperation made me nod slowly. "Tell him I'm in."

I had another message from Eli waiting when I got home. Well, Kelli did. He still wasn't talking to me.

This was probably the longest we'd ever gone without speaking, except for that time when we were about eight and I'd innocently told Billy Waters that Eli had a tea party with me the day before. Yeah, that hadn't gone over well, and he'd never had one with me again after that, no matter how much I begged and said it would be our secret.

Sighing, I clicked open the message, wondering what lovey-dovey quotes Eli would be sending the oh so perfect Kelli this time.

I still couldn't believe I was jealous of a girl who didn't even exist.

What's going on? It seems like you're trying to ignore me.

Tapping my nails on the computer's hand-rest, I tried to come up with a plausible explanation for the fact that Kelli hadn't been talking to him as much anymore.

My mom walked in the room carrying a laundry basket filled with folded clothing. "Hey, sweetie. How was your day? I didn't even hear you come home." She carried the basket over to my bed and set it down.

I lowered the screen on my laptop, and forced a carefree smile. "Oh, it was good. I went to the bookstore for a while, and then over to Sarah's."

After a moment, Mom sat down on the bed next to the laundry basket. "Is everything all right? You've been quiet at dinner the past couple of nights, and I haven't seen Eli around lately."

The smile faltered a bit. "Everything's fine." I nodded, trying to interject as much normalcy in my tone as I could. "He's been busy working on a project for school."

It was kind of obvious she didn't entirely believe me. "Are you sure? You two aren't fighting, are you?" Her eyes looked worried.

"What? Oh, no." I shook my head. "Really, everything's fine. I promise."

Mom stood up, and smoothed minute creases out of her linen slacks. "Okay, if you're positive. But you know you can talk to me if you need to." She walked over and kissed the top of my head.

I felt awful lying to her. It seemed like that was all I did anymore, lie to the people around me who I cared about the most. It took major effort to push the guilt down so it didn't swallow me whole.

"I know, Mom. Thanks." I looked directly into her eyes and added, "I love you." That part was true, at least.

"I love you too, Emma." Headed to the door, she added, "Dinner will be ready in about twenty minutes."

"Okay, thanks."

I turned back to the computer after she left the room, determined to send Eli a message that would somehow convince him to stop emailing Kelli. I couldn't keep the double identity up much longer, it was way too difficult. And it'd become clear that I had about the same chance of getting the two of us together as I did becoming bffs with Carissa.

The cursor blinked repeatedly in the blank message square. Finally, I began to type.

Eli, I'm sorry if you felt I was ignoring you. I was sick, but I guess there was more to it than that, and I wasn't sure what to say.

I still wasn't. I felt like crap for even playing games with him in the first place, but I didn't know how to stop the avalanche, so, I continued. I had to present it kindly; I didn't want Eli to be hurt by even a fake girl. He deserved so much better than that.

I guess I felt bad since I know you and I have been talking for a while, and you seem like such a nice guy. But, the thing is, I wasn't sure how you felt about me. Then I met someone recently, and we went out a couple of times. And now, I just don't feel right about talking to you when I'm dating him. I know you and I never really discussed anything like that, but I have to be honest. I think you're cute, and funny and sweet. And I don't want to confuse things by continuing to get closer to you when I'm with someone else. Maybe if I had known where things stood with us, this wouldn't have happened…who knows?

I paused a minute, closing my eyes. Why did ending things online with him seem so much like a real goodbye?

Maybe I never should have sent the friend request to you. I don't know? But I see now, this with us just isn't a good idea. I'm sorry.

It felt as though I wrote the last section from me, not Kelli. But it seemed to fit either way.

I hope you find someone great too. You deserve that.

I couldn't resist adding,

Who knows? The perfect girl could be closer than you think.

My chest tightened as I typed the last line. I wondered if there was any way that would ever come true, that he would ever look at me that way. I doubted it, especially the way things stood between us now.

I'll never forget all of our talks. Kelli

I read back over the message, and hit send before I chickened out and changed my mind. It didn't look like Eli was online, so I'd have to wait to see his response. Probably better that way, I didn't know if I could take it right now if he made some big plea for Kelli to give him a chance.

A car door slammed nearby. Gauzy curtains covered the window behind me, so I brushed them aside to look.

Eli walked toward his front yard, carrying an oversized box. The muscles in his upper arms flexed under the weight. I swallowed, watching. I inched the chair closer to get a better view. Grass stains covered his jeans, and it looked like dirt or mulch streaked his arms and hands where they grasped the box. Some kind of bricks peeked out.

A freshly dug up patch of grass circled a large maple tree in his yard. After he set the box down near the overturned earth, he ran his forearm absently across his forehead, wiping away sweat. He looked tired and dirty, and totally hot.

As though he felt my gaze, he suddenly turned and faced my bedroom window, squinting against the sun. Gasping, I pulled back and dropped the curtain. I felt stupid for gawking at him while he worked, like some love-struck peeping Tom, considering we hadn't even said a word to each other in six days.

I wondered if he'd seen me.

I grimaced, and inched forward again in the chair, sliding to lean over and peek out from the side of the window. I took care not to move the curtain this time.

He still looked my way. His head cocked slightly, but his long bangs and distance shielded his eyes from my view.

I wished he would wave or something, show that he wasn't angry anymore, that he felt badly and wanted to make up, too.

Fine, one of us had to take the first step, might as well be me. One push and the curtain cleared the window. I looked directly at him, and offered a small, tentative wave.

For a second it looked like he was going to call out, but just as quickly, his face shifted, his expression going blank. Instead of acknowledgement, he simply turned and bent down, going back to his work, ignoring me.

My heart dropped, and tears threatened. He didn't care. He didn't miss me at all.

Chapter Eighteen

Emma

Sarah sent me several texts after dinner. She was pushing me to meet up with Jake later that night since Tony worked. At first, I was going to say no, since I still hoped to hear from Eli. I was also starting to second-guess the whole fake-boyfriend plan. After all, the fake profile idea hadn't exactly gone over like gangbusters.

I stalled while I tried to decide what to do, but Sarah kept insisting it was the way to go. She said I needed to let Eli know I wasn't waiting around for him to come to his senses. I am woman, hear me roar. Or at least meow.

After sending two unanswered texts to Eli asking what movie he wanted to watch for our Sunday movie-fest the next day, I finally gave in. I told Sarah to tell Jake to meet me at Roma, the pizza place in town where a lot of the high school students went to hang out on the weekend. The large Italian restaurant still had an arcade connected to the back room, which was pretty cool. If I was going to go through with it,

I may as well be seen. Let Carissa and her cronies wonder about the cute college guy sitting next to me.

Next conundrum…what does one wear on a fake date? Do I go cute and flirty, hanging out casual, or sex-kitten ready to snag her man? I finally settled on a pair of skinny jeans and a simple pale blue T-shirt. Plain Jane it is.

Now, what to do with my hair? I studied it in the mirror. Down or up? The humidity made my curls go crazy, but wearing it down would add a little feminine appeal since my outfit sure didn't do much in that department.

I spritzed some light styling spray in my curls, hoping it would help control the frizz that was sure to come. Almost as an afterthought, I reached for my favorite perfume to wear too. Never really big on makeup, I brushed some mascara on my lashes, and dabbed on some pale gloss. Rubbing my lips together, I suddenly felt nervous.

What if Jake expected me to kiss him? After all, he was in college. Maybe college guys expected more on a date…even if it was fake. Oh God, what if he expected me to put out? Hamsters ran pell-mell on a wheel in my stomach.

"Deep breaths, Em, deep breaths." And now I'd graduated to talking to myself. Perfect.

He wouldn't think that. There was no way Sarah would've set the whole thing up if Jake was some skin hound. And he knew this was just for show anyway. Besides, it wasn't like any guy had ever found me so kissable that he couldn't restrain himself, so I obviously had nothing to worry about.

I'd always imagined my first kiss would be with Eli, or hoped, anyway. In any of my fantasies about the perfect first kiss, Eli always played the leading man, which was obviously never going to happen, so I needed to get over it. Heck, maybe if Jake tried to kiss me, I'd let him, at least then I would know what it was like. I was probably the only junior in school that had never been kissed, which made my parents' sex-talk all the more ludicrous.

My cell beeped. Sliding it out of the pocket of my jeans, I expected it to be Sarah offering some last minute advice. A part of me still held hope that it was Eli.

I didn't recognize the number on the incoming text.

Hey girl, how about I give you a ride rather than meet you there?

It had to be Jake. Before I could type a polite refusal, another message appeared.

After all, wouldn't that be a little more realistic?

Hmm. He had a point. Before I could talk myself out of it, I typed back,

Sure, thanks. 8:00 good?

His response was almost immediate.

Yep, works for me. See you soon. :)

There was a smiley. What did that mean? The whole thing was getting too awkward for words. I was over-analyzing a freaking smiley face.

I shoved the phone back into my hip pocket, and told myself to calm down. So what if this was only my second date…ever. And the first one wasn't even worth counting. I'd consider it a practice run, kinda like the PSATs.

But I couldn't completely convince myself not to feel sort of depressed, to wish I was going on a real date with someone who asked me out because he *wanted* to. Because he liked me.

It's not like I wanted Jake to feel that way, but someone.

You mean Eli, my inner cynic taunted, which was true, but at this point, even a stand-in who actually wanted to date me would be better than someone who was doing his roommate's sister a favor.

I stood up and told myself to stop whining and get over it already. This might work to get me what I really wanted. And if not? Well, maybe it was time to give up my dream of ever getting together with Eli.

The alarm clock next to my bed read 7:44. He'd be here soon. I grabbed a cropped ivory crocheted cardigan from my closet, and wondered if I should throw it on too. It might add some cute factor to an otherwise boring outfit. Then again, it might still be too warm to wear it.

I finally decided to switch the T-shirt for a lace cami so that way I could still wear the sweater and not end up sweating to death. After yanking off the T-shirt, as I pulled the wine colored cami over my head, I realized I was now messing up my hair. Awesome.

Maybe not dating was better. Sitting home alone in PJs and reading began to sound preferable. So much less stressful.

It was too late to cancel, so I licked my fingers and smoothed the flyaway hairs the best I could. It wasn't like it really mattered anyway.

A patterned hobo bag hung over the back of my desk chair, and I grabbed it and threw in my wallet and a lip-gloss. That was probably all I'd really need.

I walked over to my bedroom door, peeking out the window as I passed. Eli's car still sat parked in the driveway from earlier, but there was no sign of him. Sighing, I flipped the light switch before walking out of the room to head downstairs. I'd wait outside for Jake to show up, and avoid any questions that way.

Mom and Dad sat in the living room watching an old episode of *Lost*. Dad loved the show, and owned all six seasons on DVD. I was pretty sure Mom only put up with his obsession since she got to watch Jack run around shirtless.

"Hey! Where are you off to?" Dad hit pause and turned

to face me.

"Oh, I'm just going out with some friends over to Roma." Explaining that I was going with a guy they'd never heard of before didn't seem like a wise move.

Mom eyed my outfit. "Is Eli going, too?"

Awkward.

"Um, no. I'm not sure what he's up to tonight. I'll probably be meeting Sarah there though." I had become far more fluent at lying than I liked.

A *knock* sounded on the front door.

Jake was early. I hadn't even heard him pull up. Mom and Dad both looked at me.

"Is that Sarah?" Mom asked. "Is she picking you up?"

I closed my eyes for a few seconds, desperately thinking of some explanation. The knock came again.

Dad started to rise from the sofa. "Should I get that?" His eyebrows squished together in confusion.

"No!" I held my hands up, stopping him. "No, I'll get it. Look, I'll see you guys later, okay? Good night. Love you!" I rushed to the door before either of them could answer me.

I pulled the door open just enough to squeeze out, then quickly closed it. Jake backed up a few steps as I rushed out, almost running into him.

"Hi." He laughed at my expression of panic.

"Let's go." I grabbed his arm and began pulling him down the porch steps.

"Whoa. What's going on?" He allowed me to lead him toward his car, although his face showed a mixture of amusement and confusion. His forehead wrinkled over his twinkling eyes, and the corners of his mouth turned up in a small grin.

"Nothing. I just thought it would be good to get going, that's all."

He stopped a few steps away from his hunter green

Explorer.

"Emma, while I'm flattered you're apparently so anxious to get me alone," he said wryly, raising an eyebrow, "what's *really* going on?"

I dropped my hand from where I had practically ripped off his shirtsleeve with my tugging and stood motionless, not answering him. I shifted the strap of my purse on my shoulder, stalling as I tried to figure out what to say.

He stood patiently, waiting silently.

Finally, I decided to be wild and crazy and go with the truth. "It's just that I didn't know what to say to my parents about going out with you."

I paused.

He still didn't say a word.

"I haven't dated a lot," I blurted out quickly. "And I figured my mom and dad would've probably wanted to know who you were, how I knew you, that kind of thing." I felt like a stooge. Any minute he was going to hop back in his car and hightail it out of there.

Instead, he leaned one arm against the SUV, his eyes not leaving my face as he waited for me to continue.

"And I guess I didn't know how to answer that without looking like an idiot about all of this." I gestured toward him. "And I didn't want them to worry."

I dropped my eyes. Any moment he was going to say he didn't really want to go through with the whole thing, and I wouldn't blame him one bit.

"Emma." He paused, and when I couldn't face him, he reached a hand out and rested it under my chin, lifting it up, gently forcing me to meet his gaze. His eyes were warm, understanding, not angry at all. "You don't look like an idiot at all. In fact"—a slow smile slid across his face—"*I'd* say you look very beautiful."

He called me beautiful. No one had ever called me that

before. Well, not a guy, anyway. My breath caught, and I bit my lip, suddenly embarrassed, even though it did make me feel warm inside to hear the words.

"Well, hi there, Emma. Who's your friend?"

Chapter Nineteen

Eli

She hadn't been kidding. The feelings of jealousy that ripped through me at the sight of Emma standing next to some strange guy shocked me.

Who the hell was he?

The color drained from Emma's face when I asked about her "friend." She clearly hadn't seen me approach. Chunks of guilt snuck in as her expression turned nervous. The decent thing would have been to quietly walk inside, and not say a thing. But the words had popped out before I could stop them.

A muscle in the guy's jaw twitched almost imperceptibly, and even from where I stood I caught a knowing look cross his eyes. Apparently *he* knew who *I* was. How nice for him.

Even so, he didn't take his paws off Emma's face, or even look away from her. Instead, he actually brushed his thumb against her cheek while giving her this smarmy seductive half-smile. It spoke of possession.

I wanted to knock the smug smile off his face and tell him

to get his hands off my girl.

The thought jolted me, but it was the truth, and I couldn't deny it any more. I wanted to be with Emma with every fiber of my being. And seconds later, a more rational thought crashed in—Emma wasn't my girl. I'd blown it.

I wanted to kick myself for ignoring the texts she'd sent asking if we were still hanging out for movie night. For ignoring her when she'd waved. I'd just been so hurt and angry about her stupid double date comments, especially after she'd sent the latest messages on Facebook. There was no doubt in my mind anymore that Kelli was really Emma. I wasn't sure why she'd done it. Or why she was still lying to me.

And now…now it looked like I was too late.

I swallowed, not able to believe what was happening. I couldn't speak, so I offered Emma a hollow smile when she finally turned to face me.

She looked beautiful. The jerk was right about that. I hated him for saying it when I'd never told her. I hated myself for never telling her.

Well, I had. Once. But she didn't even know I'd meant it for her…so it didn't count. Not really. Not in the way that mattered.

And I hated that she was standing next to someone else.

"Eli. Hi. Um, this is Jake." She motioned toward the guy, who still stood mere inches away from her. Nausea crashed through me.

I couldn't blink. Couldn't say a word. I could only stare.

"Hon, we should probably get going."

Hon?

Only then did this Jake person turn his head to acknowledge me officially. "Nice meeting you." He actually mock-saluted.

My fists clenched at my sides. I'd never been a violent person, but looking at his cocky face, I was rethinking that stance.

I was acting like an ass, not talking to her, encroaching on her date…I knew it, but couldn't seem to stop myself.

"We're going to Roma," Emma said. Like I wanted to know where they were going on their hot date. Or, maybe I did. I didn't even know.

Why was she doing this? And who the hell was he? And how *old* was he? He looked like someone's uncle.

When I didn't answer, Emma didn't say anything more to me. She just turned to Joe Cool and gave him a thousand watt smile. "I'm ready whenever you are."

"Great, let's go." He led her around an Explorer to the passenger side, where he opened the door and waited for her to step in before closing it with a soft *thud.*

I wanted to tell her to stop, not to go with him. But I didn't. I just stood there, watching as the jerk walked around to the driver's side, offered a final salute in my direction, and hopped in.

Chapter Twenty

Emma

I wanted to throw up.

"Keep smiling," Jake said under his breath. He turned the key in the ignition, and placed his arm along the back of my seat as he turned to back out of the driveway.

My eyes darted between Eli standing a few yards away, and Jake sitting next to me.

Jake's profile was strong, and it hit that he'd changed clothing from when I'd seen him earlier at Sarah's house. A casual button up shirt fit just slightly snug across his chest as he stretched his arm along the back of my headrest. His light brown hair barely brushed the top of his ears. He had a clean-cut look, every inch the studious, college athlete.

As we backed past Eli, he spoke again, softly. "Laugh. Show him you're having a good time."

So I did. Tilting my head back slightly, I laughed, looking right at Jake. It rang false in the confines of the Explorer, but Eli couldn't hear that.

Jake smiled at me, then tugged lightly on one of my curls as he brought his hand back to the steering wheel. "That's my girl." He winked.

We pulled out of the driveway, headed toward Roma, and somehow, with Jake smiling at me, I no longer felt quite as sick inside as I had just moments before.

This time the laughter wasn't fake. I held my stomach, finding it difficult to breathe. God, I needed this. Jake proved to be the perfect distraction from everything going on in my life. Like Sarah said, he was smart and a great conversationalist, but surprisingly, he was also really funny.

He smiled at me from across the table. We'd been playing a game. We took turns coming up with a story about the other restaurant patrons seated around us. Jake managed to add dialogue to the story as our subjects talked. His latest was a hilarious back and forth between two juiced up muscle-heads sitting a few tables away.

Wiping tears of laughter away from my eyes, I shook my head before taking a sip of soda. "That's awful. For all you know, they're both on the fast track to Harvard."

He tipped his head my way. "You may be absolutely correct. So, I'll stop." A grin threatened.

Playing with the straw in my glass, I looked at him, suddenly serious. "Why are you doing this? I mean, why'd you even agree to help me?"

He leaned back in his seat, studying me a moment. I met his gaze head-on.

Just then, a cute server sashayed over to our table, smiling at Jake and ignoring me. "Can I get you anything else?" Her nametag read "Heather." Of course it did. All the pretty girls seemed to have names like Heather or Kelli or Brittany.

Heather even leaned on the table with one arm, making sure to place her impressive cleavage at its best advantage in front of Jake.

He barely glanced up; his attention still focused on me. I felt warm inside to be the sole subject of his interest. He offered Heather a quick, polite smile. "No, we're good, thanks. Just the check is fine." She pouted a bit at the brush off and flounced away.

I couldn't quite hide my smirk.

"What?" He'd noticed my expression.

I laughed. "Nothing. Just look at you go, only here an hour and already breaking hearts."

He rolled his eyes. "That kind of show doesn't interest me in the slightest."

"What does?" I realized belatedly that might be too personal, but I was genuinely curious to learn more about him. It felt good to sit and talk with someone without feeling constantly on guard. Or trying to hide my feelings.

"What kind of girl interests me?"

I nodded, still playing with my straw.

He cocked his head. "Hmm. I guess someone who I can really talk to, and that I don't feel like I have to provide Cliffsnotes when discussing anything deeper than which celebrity is currently in rehab."

When I laughed, he went on. "Someone who isn't afraid to be herself." He shook his head. "I honestly don't know if I have a specific type. I think it's more, I'll know her when I see her." He looked directly in my eyes when he said that. I flushed a little.

Heather returned with our check, not bothering with the boob show and tell this time. She tossed the slip of paper on the table and spun away without a word.

"You ready to go?" I figured since we'd eaten, and Eli had already seen us, Jake would be ready to head home, consider his duties done for the night.

He glanced at this watch. "It's only a little after nine. Do you have to be home already?"

"Oh, no. I just figured …"

"C'mon." He stood, glanced at the check, and pulled some cash out of his wallet before placing it down on the table.

"Where are we going?"

"It's time I beat you in some air hockey. I saw a table in the back."

Now this I could do. Sarah and I played more times than I could count; he had no idea what he was in for. "You're on." I smiled wickedly.

Chapter Twenty-One

Emma

Driving home over an hour later, I shot him an accusing glare. "You could have told me that you guys have an air hockey table in the dorm."

He laughed, a deep rumbling sound. "But that wouldn't have been nearly as much fun. You were so convinced you were going to crush me."

"Yeah, especially since you let me win the first two games. Isn't that called hustling?" I raised an eyebrow.

"Nah, we weren't playing for money," he said. "Though maybe I should have placed a bet."

"Ha, I'm a poor high school student. I can't afford to make bets."

"Who said I meant money?" It was his turn to raise an eyebrow.

I shifted in my seat.

He laughed. "Oh relax. I'm just kidding. Well, mostly." He glanced my way, his expression not entirely readable.

He had to be teasing me. He knew this whole thing was just a way for me to get Eli jealous. I wasn't interested in any other guy.

But a tiny part of me whispered, *are you sure about that?*

It'd been so nice to be around someone who saw me as a girl. Who called me beautiful. I'd noticed Jake studying me a few times at the restaurant when he didn't realize I was watching. The look on his face was one of curious interest. It was flattering.

I cleared my throat, then tried to change the subject to something less confusing. "Did you see the new movie playing yet?" I motioned out the side window to the theater as we passed, its marque announcing the latest release.

He smiled. "Nope. Haven't seen it yet. You?"

"No, but I heard it's really funny."

"Well, do you want to go? Tony works again tomorrow night until ten. We could catch an early show before I meet up with him after that."

How awkward, he must have thought I was fishing for an invitation. "No, I didn't mean you had to take me."

He reached out and gently touched my hand where it rested against my left leg. "Emma, I asked because I'd like to go with you, not because I felt like I had to."

"Oh!" My cheeks turned warm.

"So? Would you like to go and see it with me?" He pulled his hand back, placing it once again on the wheel.

I didn't know what to do. Tomorrow was Sunday, movie night with Eli. Not ready to lose my chance at seeing Eli, and maybe working things out between us, I hesitantly asked, "Can I let you know tomorrow?"

Something dropped in his features; the happy glint in his eyes faded a little. But he nodded. "Sure, you can let me know."

Things felt less light-hearted the rest of the ride home.

Something had shifted slightly between us. I felt bad, and wanted things to go back to the way they were earlier in the night. Casual, fun.

As he pulled into my driveway, the porch light cast a warm glow our way. Light also shone from my parents' room; they were probably watching television or reading.

Glancing toward Eli's house, I noticed his room was dark. His Jetta was no longer in the driveway. Did that mean he was out, or in bed already?

Opening my car door, I turned to face Jake. "Thanks for tonight. I really had a nice time."

He smiled, although it didn't quite reach his eyes. They looked disappointed.

"Here, let me walk you up."

I nodded, silently thanking him. We walked toward my front door together, about six inches apart. He didn't try to touch me, seeming to respect the fact that I needed a little space.

When we reached the door, I pushed it open slightly before turning to face him. "Jake, really, thank you."

He looked deep into my eyes for a moment, then slowly leaned in. Omigod, he was going to kiss me. My eyes widened, and my heart thundered. Pin prickles of excitement and panic raced through in equal measure.

Instead of touching his lips to mine, he merely brushed a feather-soft kiss on my cheek. Pulling back just as slowly, he looked at me once again.

My cheek tingled, and my body felt slightly warm. Confused by my reaction to him, I stared back.

He smiled gently before reaching out to brush a flyaway curl from my eyes. "Good night, Emma."

I touched my cheek absently, whispering, "Good night."

He strolled down the porch steps to the driveway, looking back once. He tipped his head slightly before hopping back into his Explorer and driving into the night.

Chapter Twenty-Two

Emma

Apparently seeing me with Jake didn't bother Eli all that much, since he sure wasn't rushing out to try to make time for me himself. Guess he didn't care. It would be the first Sunday in as far back as I could remember that we didn't get together, unless one of us were away.

Sarah and Jake had each tried to get a hold of me earlier, but I'd ignored them both. I wasn't ready to answer what was sure to be a million questions from Sarah, and as for Jake? Well, I wasn't quite sure why I'd ignored him.

Last night had been confusing. When he'd kissed me, even if it was only on the cheek, I'd felt something. What, I wasn't quite sure. And until I sorted that out, it seemed like it would be easier to stay away from him.

After getting back from visiting the grandparents, Mom and Dad asked if Eli was sick since I wasn't meeting him. After my abrupt "No," they seemed to take the hint that I didn't want to talk about it, and left me alone.

By about seven o'clock, I needed to get out of the house for a little, and decided to go for a walk. After letting my mom know I was heading out, I opened the front door. And stopped abruptly.

On the front step was a single, pale pink rose with a white ribbon trailing from the long stem. Stapled to the ribbon was a small card. I looked around, but didn't see anyone. Bending down, I picked it up, and almost couldn't believe it when I read my name printed in a small, neat script in the center of the card.

It was for me. I'd never received flowers before. Well, a few times from my parents, but that wasn't the same as a rose being left on my front porch.

Shaking slightly, I opened the small envelope. I peeked around again to make sure I was still alone. Heart skipping in my chest, I read the words written for me. There were only three.

You are beautiful.

My eyes widened and I sucked in a breath. I quickly turned the card over, but the back was blank, no signature. No way of knowing who left it for me.

Tilting my head, I drew the flower to my nose and inhaled deeply. It smelled of delicious excitement, of all the romance I'd only previously read about and imagined. It was intoxicating and all mine. I held the pale rose against my chest, careful not to touch any of the thorns on the stem. The ribbon tickled my hand where it flowed down.

Someone had left me a rose, and called me beautiful. I couldn't stop the wide grin from spreading across my face.

It had to be from Jake. After all, he'd said that to me last night, and Eli had certainly never felt the need to leave me flowers in any of the ten years we'd known each other. Not even on my birthday.

Then again, Eli heard Jake say that. Maybe he really did

care, and this was his way of finally telling me that. Maybe he really did get jealous seeing me with someone else, which made him realize he liked me as more than a friend.

The unfamiliar handwriting didn't necessarily mean anything; the florist may have filled out the card.

After all, if it was from Jake, I would have heard his car. Right?

The mere fact that I had more than one possible flower-giver made me giddy, until practicality set in, and panic washed over me. If I didn't know who it was from, how was I supposed to know who to thank? Why hadn't the person signed the card?

I turned back to the house, planning to put the rose in a vase of water. A movement from the corner of my eye caught my attention.

Eli stood at his open bedroom window, watching me. I froze, waiting to see what he'd do, if he'd give a sign that he'd left the rose. About fifteen seconds passed, although it seemed longer, but he didn't motion to me, or call out.

It felt as though a piece of me I'd held on to tightly for almost as long as I could remember was starting to crack.

Finally, he gave a sad smile, dropped the curtain, and disappeared.

Later that night as I lay in bed trying to fall asleep, a million thoughts raced through my mind. Who sent the rose? What was going on between Eli and me? How did I feel about Jake? It was so much to process. And to think just a few weeks ago, I didn't have anything close to these kind of problems. In a way, life was simpler then, but I couldn't deny this was kind of thrilling too.

I'd finally told my parents about going out with Jake. I

sort of had to since they saw the rose and wanted to know who it was from. So did I.

At first, they were a little upset about the fact that I'd gone out on a date without telling them, especially since they didn't know Jake. But after I explained how Sarah's family knew him well, they'd calmed down. They still weren't crazy about the idea, especially since he was nineteen and I didn't turn seventeen for several months, but they said I could date him again as long as they met him first.

I wasn't even sure if I was going to go out with him again, so their rule was fine with me. If I did see him again, I had no problem introducing him. If not, well, then there was nothing to worry about.

It totally sucked not knowing who sent the rose. If a guy was going to give a girl a flower, the least he could do was sign his damn name to the card.

Eli had finally messaged Kelli back. He didn't say much. Just that he understood, and hoped she was happy, even if it wasn't with him.

Sighing, I flipped over and punched my pillow a few times. Obviously, my problems wouldn't solve themselves any time soon, and I needed sleep. I was sure to run into Eli the next day at school. I would just read his cues and go from there. That's all I could do.

But somehow, the last image that passed through my mind before I finally drifted off to sleep wasn't of Eli, but of Jake…leaning in to kiss me.

Chapter Twenty-Three

ELI

"Hey."

Emma stood half buried in her locker. She spun, eyes widening into chocolate orbs when she saw me. Dark smudges beneath them hinted that she hadn't slept well, either. I wondered if she'd been up late talking to Jake, or if maybe… just maybe…she'd been thinking about us. Like I had.

"Hey." She smiled back, and a rush of relief shot through me hearing her voice. I'd missed talking to her.

"I'm sorry. I've been a jerk. I …" I scuffed a sneaker against the floor and ducked my head. It felt awkward. Not sure what to do with my hands, I shoved them in the back pockets of my jeans, then realized that probably looked dumb and took them out again.

"I'm sorry, too," she said quietly. "I should have never yelled at you last week."

"So, you and that guy, huh?" I looked straight at her, hoping to find some kind of answer in her eyes. We'd always been able to read each other so well. Before.

She didn't say anything right away…and her silence, and the pain in her eyes…spoke volumes.

My chest tightened, chains wrapping around my heart, cutting off all of my air.

"We went out on one date," she finally managed.

It didn't matter. I still knew her. I knew Emma well enough to know the words she wasn't saying, and the thing was, I couldn't blame her. I'd taken her for granted, waited too long. And the fact that I could see in her eyes that she didn't want to hurt me made me love her all the more.

It slammed into me.

I loved Emma.

I closed my eyes for a moment. When I looked at her again, I fought to hide my pain, but I needed to know. "Do you like him?" My smile probably came across as half-hearted despite my best efforts.

She tucked a curl behind her ear, and it was all I could do to stop myself from reaching out to touch it. "It was just one date," she whispered, repeating herself.

"But you can't answer my question," I pointed out softly. "It's okay, I guess I don't really have the right to ask that anymore."

I needed to let her go. She deserved that. She deserved to be happy, no matter how much it ripped me apart inside. I turned away, then stopped and looked back and looked in her beautiful eyes, which were starting to fill with tears. Guilt, pain, regret—they all clawed at my heart, and I desperately wanted to turn back the clock to the time when things were still right between us.

I couldn't stop myself, I tucked a curl behind her ear. I needed to run my fingers through her hair one last time. The pain in my chest was unbearable, but I knew I couldn't hold on if it wasn't what she wanted.

"I do hope you're happy, Em." And I meant it. I turned away for good then. As I walked away, I said so quietly that I doubt she even heard me, "Even if it's not with me."

Chapter Twenty-Four

Emma

I didn't know what to say. After all, going out with Jake had just been to get Eli jealous. But somehow I wasn't entirely sure that was all it was anymore. The past week Eli had ignored me and made me feel like I didn't matter to him. I'd begun to wonder if maybe Sarah was right, that Eli really did just like having me around, some kind of adoring fangirl that he knew was always there. And I hated even thinking that way.

But the pain I'd seen in his eyes tore me up inside. And when he'd said that…

Now wait. *Why did that sound so familiar?*

It hit. That's what he'd said to *Kelli.* Was it coincidence that he'd said the same thing to both of us, or…I blanched.

"Eli! Wait!" My voice cracked and I prayed he'd hear me before he turned the corner and went into his classroom.

If he heard, he didn't acknowledge it, or turn around.

I slammed my locker door, and raced after him. I didn't care if I was breaking the "No Running in the Halls" rule. I dodged between groups of students coming the other way.

He was too far away.

"Eli, please, wait!"

Other kids turned around to stare. Several folders began shifting in my arms, until they finally fell to the ground around me, papers flying everywhere.

"Miss Kurtz!" A loud voice boomed through the hallway, calling my name. I ignored it. Reaching a hand out to balance myself against the wall so I didn't go flying, I spun around the corner, scanning for his dark head among the dozens of other students.

I finally spotted him as he entered Ms. Mills' classroom. I was too late.

Tears threatened as I leaned against the poster-covered wall—giant signs with hearts and glitter inviting juniors and seniors to *Party at the Prom*. Just seeing such a vivid reminder of what everyone else had that I didn't made me angry. I tore one down before slowly sliding down the wall until I was sitting on the floor. I buried my head against my knees, finally allowing the tears to fall.

He knew I was Kelli.

It made sense. So many of the comments he'd made. To me and to "Kelli." How could I have been so freaking blind?

I sniffled, and wiped tears with the palm of my hand, not caring in the least that I was making a spectacle of myself.

And knowing Eli, he just didn't say anything at first because he didn't want to make me feel weird about the whole thing. I clenched my fists in my hair, wanting to scream at myself. I'd completely ruined my chance with him. He'd never forgive me. He had to think I'd been playing some stupid, twisted game with his feelings. Pretending to like him.

He'd have every right to think I was a liar who used people. And how I'd acted with Jake right in front of him… rubbing it in his face. I lowered my tear-streaked face back down on my knees, wrapping my arms around my legs.

A ball of wadded up paper bounced off my head, followed by high-pitched laughter and retreating footsteps. I barely even noticed.

A firm hand grasped my shoulder. "Miss Kurtz, follow me please."

Lifting a tear-stained face, I saw Mr. Rogers, the miserable old History teacher, towering above me.

Wiping my cheeks, I slowly stood up and wordlessly allowed him to lead me to the school office.

Principal Berger folded his hands in front of him on the wide desk. Serious eyes stared down at me as I sat in one of the uncomfortable metal chairs across from him.

"Miss Kurtz, Mr. Rogers told me you were running and yelling in the halls this morning. Plus you were throwing folders around." He paused, fingers now forming a steeple. "Your behavior as of late is concerning to me. A few weeks ago, you left school grounds without permission. I let that go, since your mother assured me she would speak to you about it."

I said nothing, tapping one foot restlessly. It was hard to maintain eye contact when all I wanted to do was go home and cry.

"Do you have anything to say for yourself?" His voice was firm, although I also caught an undercurrent of concern.

I shook my head.

"Emma, if there is something going on, I'd like to help. You're a strong student, and we've never had any issues with you in the past."

"I wasn't throwing folders around," I finally responded.

"What?"

"I said I wasn't throwing folders. They fell." I looked up.

After standing up behind the wooden desk, the principal came around to sit next to me in the second metal seat.

"Is there anything you want to tell me? Help me to understand?" His warm brown eyes were kind, almost grandfatherly. Gone was the stern disciplinarian of just a few minutes ago.

"No." I shook my head again, though tears threatened to rush to the surface.

He sighed, apparently waiting to see if I'd change my mind. When I said nothing more, he nodded. "Okay. Consider this your warning. Next time will be detention."

Head bowed, hair spilling into my face, I whispered, "I understand."

"Are you okay to go back to class, or would you like to speak to one of the guidance counselors, maybe?"

I jerked my head up, eyes wide. "No!" I added in a lower tone, "No, thank you. I don't need to talk to a counselor."

He nodded again. "All right then. The secretary will give you a pass to go to your classroom."

Rising, I pasted a half-smile on my face. "Thank you," I responded dully, before walking out to collect my pass.

I had to make it through the rest of the day somehow. Maybe I could get Eli to talk to me, to listen. The thought of losing him for good was unbearable.

As I stepped off the school bus down the block from my house, a light rain began to fall. It fit my mood, as though even the sky felt my pain and was crying for me, since I'd run out of tears hours ago.

The loud metal *swoosh* of the door closing behind me seemed to mimic my life. Sounds carried through the open bus windows, happy chatter and laughter that I wanted to cover my ears and block out.

As I walked along the cracked sidewalk, I stared at the shadows cast by the giant maples looming over me. It reminded me of the first day I'd met Eli. The trees, the sidewalk, this street, the lost feeling.

Pain built in my chest until I was sure it would explode. He'd dodged me the rest of the day, not even showing up for lunch, so I hadn't been able to try to explain things to him.

Sarah had tried to cheer me up, telling me how Jake hadn't stopped talking about me since the date. Right now, I couldn't even think about that. Sure, being with Jake that night had been a lot of fun. He made me feel special.

But Eli? Eli felt like a piece of me. He'd always been there. Cutting him out of my life would be like removing an arm or a leg. I couldn't even imagine it. But the way things stood, I also couldn't imagine how he would ever forgive me so we could move past all the crap I'd done. I wished I'd never sent that freaking, stupid friend request.

I looked up hopefully as I passed his driveway. No sign of his car. Closed garage door, so no way to tell if he was home. I thought about going up to his door and knocking, but fear stopped me. Maybe I should give him a little time.

I'd hurt him, and he probably thought the latest messages from Kelli were how *I* felt, that I didn't want to see him anymore, especially after the little show Jake and I put on in front of him in the driveway.

I pulled my front door open. Crawling into bed sounded perfect. Offering a half-hearted wave to my dad as I passed the kitchen, I called out, "I'm going to get started on my homework." I didn't want him to know anything was wrong.

"Do you want a snack?" His voice carried my way as I hit the stairs.

"No, I'm good, but thanks." I yelled back over my

shoulder.

As I entered my room and dropped the heavy book bag on the floor inside the door, my eyes traveled to the closed laptop. I moaned. The whole plan caused nothing but trouble.

Maybe I should try to message him through Facebook. He'd been willing to go along with it, even knowing the truth. Maybe he'd still listen that way. I needed him to understand what I did, and why I did it.

I walked over to my desk and sat down. Opening the computer, I navigated to Kelli's page and signed in. Just seeing it filled my mouth with a sour taste. To my surprise, there was already a message waiting for me. From Eli. He must have written it as soon as he got home from school.

Hands trembling, I moved the mouse to click it open.

> *I'm done with the games. I'm not going to pretend I'm not hurt. I am. I don't understand why you would have done all of this just to go and date someone else. Maybe it is for the best though. Maybe we're just too close as friends to try to cross into something else. Maybe it's my fault for not realizing what might have been possible sooner. But right now, I need some time. I need to figure out what's going on in my head, and you need to figure out what's going on in yours too. Because I saw the way he looked at you. And more importantly, I saw the way you looked at him when he dropped you off. You always looked at me like you cared, but never like that. And that's probably my fault too. No matter what happens, I'll always be here for you. Eli.*

I burst into tears. Because it felt like a goodbye, no matter what he said. I also cried because deep down, I was afraid he might be right.

Chapter Twenty-Five

Emma

Curled up in bed later that evening, I tried to watch television, but couldn't focus on anything on the screen. I pulled my thin sheet up around me, needing the comfort. Dusk outside, the moon only started to shine through the burnt sky. Crickets chirped in the yard, and a light breeze blew the curtains gently away from the screens in the window next to my bed.

My parents had gone to a friend's house for drinks after dinner. They rarely went out just the two of them, and I was relieved tonight was one of their rare couple-nights. I didn't want to face their worried looks.

Thirsty, I padded downstairs to get a bottle of water. I'd slipped into a pair of navy cotton shorts and one of Eli's old baseball T-shirts. It hung ridiculously loose on me, but I loved it. One of my favorite sleep-tees, the letters of his last name and team number on the back had long ago faded from so many washings. He'd lent it to me about two years ago after we'd had a water fight in his back yard. I'd never given it back.

Just as I twisted the plastic cap off, the doorbell rang. I froze.

Maybe Mom and Dad left the party already, and forgot their house key or something. It seemed pretty early for them to be back, but I sure wasn't expecting anyone. The kitchen tile chilled my bare feet as I tiptoed toward the door, gulping down some water on the way.

After pulling the door open, surprise made me choke on a mouthful of water.

Jake stood on the front step, his smile turning to alarm as I kept hacking in his face.

"Are you okay?"

I held up the water bottle, nodding my head and holding up the index finger on my other hand in the universal "just a second" signal.

Jake gallantly reached behind me to thump my back a few times, rather than simply running to his car at the sight of my bulging eyes and the dribbles running down my chin.

Clearing my throat after the coughing fit finally diminished, warmth crept up my neck as he watched me. "I'm fine. Thanks." I choked out, looking at him curiously. "What are you doing here?"

When he shifted uncomfortably on his feet, it occurred to me how rude that probably sounded. "I'm sorry, I didn't mean it like that. I'm just surprised to see you, that's all."

He looked relieved. His face relaxed, and the warmth returned to his eyes. "I tried calling you a couple of times," he said. "When I didn't hear back, I guess I got worried that I did something wrong. I didn't know if you were upset with me for…" He rocked back and forth on his feet, not quite facing me. "For kissing you the other night." He cleared his throat and finally looked directly at me.

"No, I'm not mad at you." *Brilliant, Em.* I smiled, hoping he would realize I was glad he stopped by.

He grinned. "Well, that's a relief." He glanced around, adjusting the baseball cap on his head. "Um, can I come in?"

"What? Oh, sorry!" I stammered, embarrassed that I'd made him stand at the door like he was selling something. I waved him inside. "Sure, c'mon in."

Just as he began to step forward, I suddenly jerked my hand out to his chest, blocking him. "Wait! No. I don't know if you should."

His eyes widened and his brows drew together.

"It's not that I don't want you to come in, but my parents aren't home. And I don't know if they'd like finding a guy they never met here in the house with me when they get back," I said, feeling ridiculous. Plus, I had to fight the impulse to look and see if Eli was anywhere in sight. If he saw Jake at my door, it would most likely only cause more problems between us.

I wasn't sure what I was supposed to do, let alone what I wanted to do. A part of me felt a tiny rush seeing Jake again, knowing I mattered enough for him to stop by to see me. But another part felt guilty even having those feelings.

He stepped back again. "Oh. Okay. Well, do you want to go for a drive? Or a walk? Would that be okay?"

I'd worried that someone in college wouldn't want to be bothered dealing with something as annoying as parental rules. I couldn't help but be flattered that it didn't seem to distract him from wanting to spend time with me.

"Um…I can't." I said softly. Sighing, I went on. "After last time, my mom and dad said if I went out anywhere with you again, they wanted to meet you first." I offered an embarrassed smile. "They were a little worried because they don't know you, and you're older than I am. It's not that I don't want to," I rushed on. He was sure to give up and bolt now. After all, he was asking me to go for a walk, not for my hand in marriage.

Smiling a little, he asked, "Well, do you think they'd be okay if we sit on the porch and talk?"

Relief washed over me. Grinning, I nodded and motioned toward the front steps. "This okay? There's not really anywhere else to sit."

"Works for me." He walked to the top brick step and sat down, stretching his long legs out in front of him. He was dressed more casually than when we went out Saturday night, in a pair of athletic shorts and a black hoodie. Under the hat, his hair looked slightly damp.

I joined him, making sure to leave several inches of space between us. Suddenly feeling awkward about what I was wearing, I tugged self-consciously at the hem of my T-shirt.

"I'm a wreck. I obviously wasn't expecting company."

"Why do girls always think they look bad when they're dressed comfortably?"

I shrugged, and fiddled with the strands falling loose from my ponytail.

He sighed. "Emma, you look fine. Adorable, even. I like this look on you." He tilted his head and smiled. "Don't you get it? Most guys don't give a shit about all the makeup and fancy outfits. We want to know what a girl's face really looks like under the junk they paint on." He touched my cheek, "And when it looks like this? That's a good thing." He paused, staring directly into my eyes. "A very good thing," he said more softly.

My skin tingled under his touch, and my mouth went dry, despite the water I'd just drank.

He must have sensed my nervousness, because he dropped his hand. "To me, getting to know a person is kind of like getting a present. Sure, a pretty package looks nice, but I'm more interested in what's inside. The wrapping being spectacular?" He shook his head a little, considering. "Well, that's a very appreciated bonus." He grinned, his teeth shining white in the fading light.

I looked at him, trying to figure out if he was telling me

the truth or if it was just some really good come-on line. He met my gaze, his deep blue eyes seeming to convey that he meant every word. I smiled again, whispers of excitement tickling me all over. It made me feel special, wanted, to have Jake looking at me like that…saying those things to me.

I had to break eye contact before I did something stupid like jump on his lap. I took a quick sip of water and mumbled, "Sorry I didn't call you back. Things have just been kind of… weird lately. I've had a lot on my mind." I looked up again, trying to gauge his reaction.

"Can I ask a question?"

"Sure."

"The stuff on your mind, does it have to do with your neighbor? I take it he's the guy you and Sarah were talking about. The one you like so much." His jaw twitched slightly, his pulse visibly beating in his throat. "I mean, you don't have to tell me or anything, I just wondered. But you can tell me it's none of my business."

Dropping my head for a moment, I tried to figure out the best way to respond. Obviously, Eli was on my mind. But, so was Jake.

"Yeah, he's part of it." I finally answered softly. "But"—I raised my eyes, took a deep breath, and looked right at him—"So are you." I bit my lip, suddenly feeling like I needed to try to make him understand. "Maybe I should explain something," I said.

Jake sat very still, waiting for me to go on. His look was open, not judgmental.

"You see, when my family moved here ten years ago, Eli was the first friend I made. And ever since then, we did everything together."

Jake's eyes widened slightly, and I hurried on. "No, not that!" We both laughed as my cheeks turned pink. "I mean, we became best friends. From first grade, Eli was there for me no matter what."

Jake nodded.

"We told each other secrets, and played together all the time. He stood up for me if kids at school picked on me." I paused. "And eventually, I guess I began to build him up in my head to almost super-hero status."

The sky darkened around us, causing shadows from the street lamps flickering to life to fall across Jake's face.

"And you fell in love with him," he finished quietly.

I leaned back on both hands, looking out at the trees along the street. "I thought I did," I admitted. "But lately, I'm sometimes not so sure if it's love, or some kind of infatuation." I shook my head. "I'm not saying he isn't a great guy, because he is. He's the best. It's just…" I sighed. "Maybe it was more a young girl's crush that I became so used to having, I didn't look any deeper to question what I was *really* feeling. I'm not sure." I peeked over.

He was looking down at his sneakers. His face was hard to read between the night and the hat.

"Are you mad?" I suddenly felt like maybe I shouldn't have said all of that. Maybe I revealed too much. He probably didn't want to hear about my relationship with another guy. Or, maybe he was wondering why I explained so much, since whatever was going on between me and Eli didn't really concern him. Maybe I'd read too much into his feelings, thought something was there that wasn't.

I peeled the label off my bottle while I waited for him to respond.

He lifted his head to look at me before answering. "No, I'm not mad." He shifted on the step, moving slightly closer. "Emma, when I agreed to go out with you, I didn't expect anything, or any of this." He motioned to me, then himself. "I mean, when I first saw you, I obviously thought you were pretty."

The blush that was becoming way too common when I was around him began to rise again.

"But I wasn't really looking to get involved with anyone right now. At all. I'm really trying to keep my grades up, so I don't lose my scholarship." He shook his head a little. "College is different than high school, let me tell you. There's no one there to stay on your ass and make sure you're getting to class and doing your work. It's all up to you. And I really want to get into a good grad school in a few years, so I need to make sure not to let any of my grades slide."

He reached up to take his hat off, and ran his hand through his hair, messing it up a little. It made him look sexy all tousled.

"I've barely dated this year at school," he admitted. "But when I came over to pick you up, and saw you running out of the house all nervous," he laughed a little, "I don't know. Something happened. And the more we talked that night, I realized I wanted to get to know you even more. I wanted to be able to keep listening to your voice, your laugh." He suddenly stopped short.

Wow. No one had ever said anything like that to me before. It sounded like something from a movie.

"But you leave to go back right after spring break is over. Maybe us hanging out really isn't a good idea." Even as I offered up the counter argument, I was afraid that he'd agree with me, because a part of me wanted to get to know him better too.

"Well, school is only a little over an hour away. And I come back with Tony a lot since I live with my dad in New York. He's a doctor, and he does those doctors without borders trips pretty often since I graduated from high school." He messed with his hair again. "I mean, I still go back home to see him once in a while, but to tell the truth, we haven't been as close since my mom died a few years ago. It hit him really hard, and

I don't think he ever let himself to get over it. To try to move on."

"Oh Jake, I'm so sorry." I reached out and touched his hand. I couldn't imagine losing my mom, and rarely seeing my dad.

"No, it's okay. As awful as it sounds, it was better that she passed. She was in a lot of pain near the end." He swallowed visibly. "She had bone cancer. She was really great, though. I was lucky to have her as long as I did." His voice sounded hoarse. He cleared his throat, then went on, softly, "I think she really would have liked you."

I tightened my hold on his hand. "She sounds like she was an amazing person."

He dipped his head. "Yeah, she was."

A few minutes passed, neither of us saying a word. The street was quiet, with only an occasional car driving by.

"My parents will probably be home soon," I finally said, not really wanting to cut our time together short, but knowing it was probably a good idea to go inside before they got back.

"I guess I should go." He looked at my face, and I could almost feel his eyes tracing each feature—my eyes, my cheekbones, my lips. Finally he dropped his gaze down to where my hand still covered his. "Can we go out again? Maybe tomorrow?" His voice seemed hesitant, as if he still wasn't sure how I felt about the idea.

"I'd like that."

His head shot up again, his expression boyishly pleased. "Okay, great. What would you like to do? We could see a movie, or maybe play a round of miniature golf?"

"Mini-golf isn't open yet, but a movie sounds good." I smiled, a rush of excitement shooting through me. I had been asked out, on an official date.

"How about I pick you up about 6:30? That'll give us time to get there for the early show. We won't be out late that way, since I wasn't sure how your parents are about you going out on a school night."

"Actually, tomorrow we only have a half-day, then our spring break starts too."

"Oh! Well, that's even better. Maybe we can do something ahead of time in the afternoon." He sounded happy. "If you want to, that is."

"How about I'll text you when I get home, see if my mom has anything planned after school. Plus, it will give me a chance to tell them we're going out again."

He turned his hand over so our palms touched. His fingers laced between each of mine. I swallowed. It was the first time a boy had held my hand, other than Eli. And somehow with Jake, it felt different. Tiny sparks traveled from each of his fingers to mine.

"I'm really glad we're going out again."

"Me too," I whispered.

He stood up, still not releasing his hold on my hand. We stood facing each other, hands clasped. I was a little dizzy, standing close enough to feel his breath on my face. I was acutely aware of each of his fingers between mine, the feel of his palm pressing against my own, like my senses were hyperaware.

An image of the rose left on the front step crossed my mind. It had to be from him. Just as I was about to ask if he had left it for me, a car passed, and the driver blew the horn. A voice catcalled out the window, "Woo-hoooo!"

I blushed, and he chuckled. "I guess that's my cue to go." He squeezed my hand gently before dropping his hold. "I'll see you tomorrow."

"I'll see you tomorrow," I echoed. I'd ask him then.

"Goodnight, Emma."

"Night."

He walked down the steps. When he reached the bottom,

he turned back to face me. "Go in and lock up before I go. I want to make sure you get in okay since your parents aren't home yet."

Something in my heart melted a little when he said that.

I smiled at him. "I'll be fine."

"I know. Just humor me."

Laughing, I opened the door and stepped onto the threshold. "See? I'm good."

He laughed too. "Yes you are." Winking, he hopped in his car. Before he backed out, he sat, waiting for me to go inside first.

Shaking my head and smiling, I waved and began to close the door. Jake smiled wide and waved back.

"Sweet dreams!" he called out.

I couldn't help but grin. Closing the door, I turned the lock before peeking out the thin pane of glass beside the door. His taillights glowed red as he pulled into the street.

Giggling to myself, I whispered, "I have a date."

Chapter Twenty-Six

Emma

"I can't believe you're going out with him. This is so awesome." Sarah stuffed the last of a chicken wrap into her mouth and chewed, her head bouncing with each rigorous movement of her jaw. She wiped her mouth with one of the scratchy paper napkins the school so generously provided for the students. "I mean, after how long you've been mooning after Eli—"

"I wasn't mooning after him!"

Sarah rolled her eyes. "Well, whatever it makes you feel better to call it." Shoving the napkin in her now-empty milk carton, she glanced a few tables over to where Eli sat with some of his soccer buddies. "I mean, the last one with Jake wasn't exactly official, but this? This is a real date." She nodded. "But what about him?" Sarah jerked her head in Eli's direction.

I peeked over toward him too. He was half-turned on the seat, facing his friend, Kevin. There was no way to hear what he was talking about since they were too far away. Kevin was laughing at something. I wondered if it had to do with me.

Eli hadn't talked to me all morning. It was like we were taking turns playing hide and seek from each other. I hated it.

Sighing, I shook my head. "I have no idea. I feel like I should try to explain things to him, maybe make him understand?"

Sarah leaned back slightly and stared at me. "Em, it seems like you've done nothing but try to make Eli do one thing or another for weeks now. Maybe instead, it's time you realized there are some things that aren't in your power. And if you try to push too hard, something is going to slam you in the face." She stood, picking her tray up from the table, and raised her eyebrow in silent question.

"I'm coming." I got up and followed her bright T-shirt through the throngs of shoving students headed to drop their trays off before the bell rang. As I passed Eli's table, my eyes pulled in his direction.

He sat completely still, as though he knew I was there and didn't want to acknowledge my presence. His Flyers jersey had a blob of mustard on the front, which ridiculously caught my attention.

Biting my lip, I considered what to do. I could continue on my way and pass by without saying anything, since it was obvious he didn't want to speak to me. Or, I could confront him, beg him to talk if it came to that.

My hands tightened around the edges of the brown plastic tray. Pressing my lips together, I took a step in his direction, then stopped. Kevin spotted me and nudged Eli. When he looked up, our eyes met for one never-ending second, until he dropped his gaze, choosing to stare at his bottle of green tea instead of acknowledge me.

Straightening my shoulders, chin held high, I continued on my path to his table. As I approached, I cleared my throat. Kevin snickered. I gave him a clear "drop dead" look before tapping Eli on the shoulder.

He may be upset, but he wasn't the type to be flat-out rude. Turning his head, he once again looked at me, his eyes a kaleidoscope of color and emotion. "Hey," was all he offered.

"Hey." My voice shook a little. "I was wondering if we could talk."

Eli glanced around his table, then at the large white clock on the far wall. "The bell's going to ring any minute."

Shaking my head, I corrected, "No, I didn't mean now. Can we talk after school?" When he didn't answer, I continued, more softly, "Please, Eli?"

His eyes locked on mine for a fraction of a second. Usually so good at reading him, this time, I was clueless.

"Yeah, okay. We don't have drills today because of getting out early, so I'm leaving right after dismissal. If you meet me by my car, I'll give you a ride home." He paused. "We can talk then. Does that work for you?" His voice was cool, polite. It ripped me to shreds, but at least he was speaking to me.

I nodded, "That's fine. I'll see you then."

But he'd already turned away.

Sarah stood over by the tray drop, waiting for me with a disapproving expression. "You're making this all worse," she said as I approached and deposited my tray on top of the tilting stacks in the gray bin.

"Sarah, please. Can you try to understand? This is Eli we're talking about. I can't ignore him and pretend none of this happened. I already get that I screwed things up, okay?" Tears welled up, and I fought to keep them at bay in the crowded cafeteria. "I did this. *Me.*" I slammed my palm against my chest so hard it stung. "I know everything that happened the past couple of weeks is my fault, but now I have to at least try to fix it, try to explain to him that I wasn't doing it to be a bitch." I trembled.

"I'm sorry. You're right." Sarah reached out and tugged

on my sleeve, maneuvering me toward the double doors leading from the cafeteria to the hallway. "Come on, let's go to the bathroom and get you fixed up."

A tear crept down the side of my face, despite my best efforts to hold it back. *Please don't let him be looking.* I forced a fake smile, and nodded, walking as fast as I could without looking like a complete fool trying to escape humiliation.

"Almost there," Sarah whispered. "Just talk to me. I don't care what you say. You don't want to give Eli or those guys anything to talk about."

I nodded again, and began reciting the alphabet half under my breath in Sarah's direction, hoping it appeared to anyone looking our way like we were have a completely normal conversation. I'd become adept at idiocy.

Just when I thought I was safe, the door only steps away, a sickeningly sweet voice behind me called out, "Oh, Emma! Here, do you need a tissue?" Followed by titters. Carissa. Of course.

Normally, I would ignore the taunting, but I was past that point. I turned, facing the other girl head-on. Carissa dangled a Kleenex in my direction, smile mocking. Her eyes glinted sharply, like a snake right before it strikes.

Instead of allowing myself to feel intimidated, I reached out and grabbed the Kleenex. Before I could stop myself, I shoved it down the front of Carissa's low-cut baby-doll T-shirt. "There. I figured you can add this to your fake boobs, Carissa. You know, less danger of puncturing one if you use protection."

A snort burst out of Sarah, before turning into a full-fledge laugh.

"And just so you know? *You're* the one who doesn't have a shot with him. You're the joke."

Carissa's china-blue eyes widened, false lashes expanding out to look like some alien tarantula. Her mouth formed a giant "O," but nothing came out.

Sarah and I turned and walked away, ignoring the amused looks on the students around us. "That was *epic*!" Sarah cheered, giving me the thumbs up.

"The look on her face was priceless." She shook her head. "Damn girl, you've finally grown a set of balls."

Cheeks flushed, I giggled as I walked toward my locker, a mixture of pride and fear encompassing me. "Maybe I shouldn't have done it. She's really going to have it in for me now, especially saying that about Eli to her."

Sarah shrugged. "So what's new? She's always been jealous of you two, I told you that for years. At least now she knows you aren't going to sit back and take it anymore."

"I guess." I turned the combination on my locker, anxious for the day to be over. There was just final homeroom to get through. "I didn't even get a chance to tell you. I'm meeting Eli after school. He said he'd give me a ride home and we could talk."

The bell rang, signaling students had three minutes to get to their classrooms. Sarah raised her eyebrows. "Well, call me afterward. I wanna know how it goes."

"I will."

"And sweetie?" She paused, concern etching her features before she shook her head. "Never mind." She offered a quick wave as she sped off to get to her own locker and make it to end of day homeroom before the late bell.

As students milled around me, laughing and talking, I rested my head against the closed locker. The metal was cool against my still-flushed skin. Now I only had to figure out what to say to Eli. Unfortunately, I didn't have a clue where to begin.

Eli sat behind the wheel, fingers drumming absently, as I walked toward his car after classes. He looked as nervous as I felt.

My stomach churned like the time I had a bad flu last spring. Things had changed so much between us, and it was all my fault. This wasn't at all what I'd imagined when I plotted the whole thing out weeks ago. In my mind, we would have been closer than ever by now. We were supposed to be telling each other how happy we were that I'd brought us together in between heated bouts of kissing. It hadn't gone down even close to that scenario.

Shifting my book bag off my shoulder until I held the wide straps in my hand, I licked my lips and rapped on the window lightly before opening the car door. His hands paused beating the tempo on the steering wheel, and he looked up. Just seeing his familiar face sent my heart racing.

"Thanks for the ride," I said, sliding in and stuffing my bag on the scuffed floor mat between my feet.

His eyes followed my movements. "Sure," he said, voice low. It was clear he felt as uncomfortable with the situation as I did.

After I closed the door and put on my seatbelt, I stilled, wishing there was something to do with my hands to cover the awkwardness. I cleared my throat when Eli simply sat back, also not moving. "Um…should we go?" I asked.

"Oh, yeah." He turned the key in the ignition and pulled forward, nearly mowing over a student walking in front of his car in the process. Slamming on the brakes, he pressed his lips together, muffling a curse. "Sorry about that." He glanced my way.

"It's okay."

This was worse than I thought. It was clear neither of us knew how to bring up what was on both of our minds.

He looked ahead, pulling out much more slowly this time.

I tried to come up with a good way to start the conversation.

"I'm sorry," I said.

A muscle in his jaw twitched, but he said nothing.

"Eli, please."

His head jerked slightly in my direction. "Please what, Em? Please say it's all okay? Please understand why you made up a profile and pretended to be some girl rather than just talking to me?" His hands clenched on the wheel. "Or, maybe, please be cool with you flaunting some strange guy in front of me who you're now suddenly dating." He met my stare for a moment. "So tell me, Em. Please what?"

The breath whooshed out of me at the pain and anger in his tone. I wasn't sure how to respond to all he'd thrown at me.

He rubbed his eyes, shaking his head. "Why, Em? Just tell me why. I don't understand any of this. I don't."

What had I done? How could I have ever caused this rift between the two of us? I felt sick, really and truly sick at the mess I'd caused, at the pain in his eyes. Could it be that Sarah was wrong, that Eli really returned the feelings I'd held for so long? What if I'd made the biggest mistake of my life by agreeing to go on the date with Jake?

The buildings and people we passed driving home were a blur. The only thing that mattered was what was happening right here in the car…with Eli.

"How did you know it was me?"

He snorted. "Please. That first night when you almost took off my fingers, I saw the profile before you slammed your computer lid down. I was pretty sure it was 'Kelli's.'" He made air quotes with one hand. "That seemed weird, since I hadn't even told you about it. But, at first I thought maybe you noticed I added her and you were checking it out." He rolled his eyes. "But then, little things you said here and there seemed off. Plus, the profile was just a little too much like you."

Silence fell.

"Who's the guy?" he finally asked.

"A roommate of Sarah's brother. They go to school together."

He nodded slowly. "And what? You two are suddenly going out?"

"Well…" I stopped. "It's kind of hard to explain."

He turned onto our street. "How hard can it be? Are you dating?"

I swallowed. "Look, can we talk about the rest of this inside?"

Nodding, he slid into his driveway and shut off the car. "Yeah, sure," he muttered. "I can't wait to hear all about it."

"Eli. It's not like that."

"Really? Then what *is* it like?" He yanked the keys out of the ignition.

I reached out, tentatively, then dropped my hand. "Can we go inside?"

He nodded again, and sighed. "Yeah. Look, I'm sorry. I'm …" He shook his head. "I don't even know for sure what I am right now." He stared vacantly out the windshield. "Do you want to come in or go to your place?"

"Whichever you want is fine." I was afraid to say too much, to jinx the tentative road to restoring things between us that seemed to exist right now.

"How about I'll go in and check Vader, then I'll be over in about ten minutes?"

"Sounds good." I paused. "And Eli?" He looked up at me, his eyes searching out my own. "Thank you."

He smiled, a soft, sad smile like he knew something I didn't. He only nodded before turning to get out of the car.

Well, it was a start anyway. We'd obviously have a lot of talking to do. Hopefully, it wouldn't make things any worse. I didn't see how it could.

Chapter Twenty-Seven

Emma

When I walked into the house, I listened for my dad. No discernable noises came from his office. He usually had the radio set low to a jazz station when he was in there. No sign of my mom either, although she usually got home an hour or so after me, since she stayed after school to finish up paperwork.

It was probably better this way, no chance of either of them popping in the room while Eli and I talked.

Dumping my stuff at the bottom of the steps, I wandered into the kitchen to grab something to drink. My stomach growled, reminding me that I hadn't eaten much at lunch. Reaching out to open a cabinet, I rooted through the contents trying to figure out what I wanted to take upstairs for us to snack on. In the midst of reaching for a packet of popcorn, a wave of nostalgia hit. We always ate popcorn on movie nights. Maybe the talk would go better than expected and we could have one tonight to make up for missing it on Sunday.

Tonight.

I was supposed to be going out with Jake tonight. I'd promised to call or text him when I got home. He'd mentioned about maybe getting together in the afternoon since there was only a half-day today at school. What if he decided to show up and Eli was still here?

I frantically felt for my phone in my jeans pocket, but it wasn't there. Running back over to the landing, I ripped open the front pocket of my book bag, searching for the phone. I found it stuffed between a paperback copy of *The Fault in our Stars* and *Hamlet*. I pulled it out, pressing buttons wildly, willing him to pick up, and fast. I walked over to the front window and peeked out, hoping Eli didn't show up early.

Just as I was about to hang up, thinking he wasn't going to answer, his cheery hello sounded in my ear.

"Jake! Hey, it's me, Emma."

"Hey, beautiful. I was waiting for your call. Sorry it took me so long to pick up, I was in the middle of trying to wash oil off of my hands. I was helping Tony—"

I interrupted him, feeling awful about being so rude, but nervous that I was running out of time. "Jake, I'm sorry, but I have something I have to do right now that just came up, so I might not be able to call you to figure out what's going on tonight until later." My words came out rushed.

"Okay," he said slowly. "Is everything all right?"

I could hear the confusion in his voice, and I didn't blame him. Doing this to him after yesterday…I was a grade-A bitch.

"Everything's fine. I just…I have to do something right now."

When he spoke again, his voice was slightly cooler than before. "Emma, if you've changed your mind, that's fine. You can tell me."

"No, it's not that I've changed my mind. It's only, I have to…" I trailed off, feeling awful for admitting what I was doing.

"Let me guess. This has something to do with your neighbor, doesn't it?" He didn't sound angry, just resigned.

"I need to talk to him. That's all." I was the biggest creep in the world. All I did anymore was make everyone mad, or hurt. "Please try to understand."

"I do. Maybe better than you realize."

I peeked out the window again. Eli still hadn't come out of his house.

"Why don't you call me when you're done. Let me know if you still want to get together, okay?"

I definitely felt like a shit.

Nodding even though he couldn't see me, I answered, "I will. I'm sorry. Please don't be mad."

"I'm not. I hope you figure out whatever you need to." He paused, and when he spoke again, his voice was soft, and held a world a meaning in two simple words. "Bye, Emma."

"Bye." But he was already gone.

The whole thing was turning into such a mess. I didn't know what to do, or what to think. Did I want to still go out with Jake? Or was he just a distraction since I couldn't have Eli? I was so confused.

Part of me felt awful about pushing Jake away, even though I'd promised to call him later. He'd been nothing but nice to me. He made me feel special, pretty. He was fun to hang out with, and he made me laugh.

On the other hand, well…it was *Eli*. He'd always been there for me, through the good and bad. He helped me bury my pet goldfish when I was nine, and went with me to visit Nana and Pap, and he…well, he was like my other half. I couldn't imagine walking away from that. And somehow I couldn't see things staying the same between the two of us if I actually went through with going on a date with someone else.

But maybe they aren't supposed to. Maybe things aren't

supposed to stay the same.

I pushed aside the niggling doubt trying to force its way into my mind. I couldn't bear to think about that right now.

Stuffing the phone into my back pocket, I went back into the kitchen to put the popcorn I had left on the counter back into the cupboard. I was pretty sure we wouldn't be needing it. Sighing, I turned to the refrigerator and opened it. Milk, water, OJ, and a few cans of soda. I reached in and grabbed two Dr. Peppers.

Just as I turned to head to my room, the front door opened. It was probably him. Neither of us felt the need to knock at each other's houses anymore after years of coming and going between them.

I called out, "I'm in the kitchen!"

Footsteps approached, and then he was standing in the doorway. My heart lurched seeing him. The same familiar pull I experienced every time he entered a room hit me.

His jeans were faded, nothing fancy. He'd changed his shirt. I noticed he didn't have the jersey with the mustard stain anymore. Instead, he was wearing one of my favorites, a black fitted T-shirt that showed off his abs to perfection.

I gulped. Did he know how much I liked him in that? Was that why he wore it? Telling myself that I was reading way too much into him simply changing his shirt, I willed my heartbeat to slow back down to a normal rhythm.

"Here." I abruptly shoved a can of soda in his direction.

He cocked his head, studying me. "Um…thanks." A faint smile crept over his features, and when he reached out to accept it, his fingers brushed mine on the cold can. I jerked my hand back as if I'd been stung, and the soda flew to the ground. It bounced twice before rolling a few feet away to rest under the bottom ledge of the counter.

He raised his eyes from the can to look at me. His scrutiny caused me to hold my breath. I expelled it when I realized what I was doing. "I'm sorry. That was an accident."

His smile was back, accompanied by a twinkle in his eyes. "I figured."

"Here, let me get you another. That one will probably explode if you try to open it." I turned to head toward the refrigerator again, anything to keep him from seeing how flustered I felt.

A hand on the side of my waist stopped me. I completely froze. Every cell in my body glowed, vividly aware of the feel of his hand, his fingers just a breath away from touching my bare skin where my shirt didn't quite meet my jeans. Tingles spread from my waist through my hip and shot in pathways over my entire body. My mouth became a scorched desert.

"Em." His voice was low, husky, filled with emotion.

Just my name. That's all he said, and it was enough. I didn't even need more words at that point, but I couldn't turn around, couldn't look at him, afraid too much would show on my face—everything I'd felt for so long.

The pressure on my waist increased, pulling me around. As I turned, his hand dropped, only to be replaced on my other hip once I faced him. He didn't move closer, he still stood an arm's reach away, but his hand against my right hip burnt through my jeans. I might as well have been naked for how exposed I felt.

I reminded myself to breathe and stared at his sneakers. One frayed lace was loose.

"Why won't you look at me?" His voice was soft.

I closed my eyes and shook my head.

He sighed. "Come here." He stepped closer, getting rid of the extra space between us. A fraction of a second later, he reached both of his strong arms around my shoulders and pulled me to him. His heartbeat pounded against my chest. He held me tight, running a hand through the hair spilling down my back.

Unable to resist, I wrapped my arms around his neck and allowed myself to fall into the moment, to feel his strength, his comfort, his caring. I rested my head against his shoulder, breathing him in.

"I've missed you," I whispered.

His lips were a breath away from my ear as he leaned down to whisper, "I missed you, too."

A small tear ran down my cheek. Those seconds in his arms felt perfect. They felt like home.

We stood that way for several minutes, not speaking, just holding each other. His hand traced patterns against my back, sure and familiar.

Eventually, he pulled back slightly to look down at my face. He smiled. "Your makeup stuff is all smeared under your eyes."

I rubbed my eyes self-consciously. He laughed quietly, watching. We were still close enough that I felt the rumble of his laughter against my middle.

Starting to laugh too, I swatted him on the arm. "Oh stop it. It's not nice to mock my messy face."

He suddenly turned serious. "I would never mock you, Em. Ever. And I don't care if you have smudged makeup. You're—"

"Emma, you home?" My father's voice called from down the hall. The front door hadn't opened; he must've been here the whole time.

Eli dropped his arms, and took a quick step backward.

Wait, what had Eli been about to say? I was...*what?* Of all the times for Dad to decide to come looking for me.

I rubbed more forcefully underneath my eyes, hoping to erase any traces of runaway make-up or tears.

"Hey, Dad! We're in the kitchen." I bent down to pick up the can that got away earlier.

My father stepped into the room, reading glasses perched

atop his head, holding a sheaf of papers.

"Hey, honey." His eyebrows rose as he took in the scene. "Eli!" He sounded surprised. "Well, son, you haven't been around in a while. It's nice to see you." Dad walked in and clapped Eli on the back, smiling.

I bit back a grin. Dad always liked Eli, and it hadn't taken a genius to see it'd driven him nuts when I cut off any questions about Eli's absence recently.

Eli smiled, then shifted a little under the attention. "Thank you, sir."

Rolling my eyes at the man-theatrics, I reached out the can toward Eli. "It should be safe by now."

"Thanks." He winked. "Again."

"So how are your folks doing? I haven't seen them much lately."

"Oh, they're good. They got back from California a few weeks ago. They had that business trip to help promote Mom's work. It went well. A few more shops will be carrying her stuff."

Eli's mom designed gorgeous stained-glass artwork, and his dad, some type of business know it all, helped her launch into consigning it at some upscale boutiques. Her art sold as quickly as she could make it.

Dad nodded. "Good for them, happy to hear it. Well, tell them they need to make time and we'll have a barbeque soon, okay?"

"I will." Eli shuffled his feet and glanced at me. I smiled and offered him a silent *cheers* with my soda. He grinned and popped the top of his own and took a long swallow. I instructed myself not to stare at his throat moving, the moisture on his lip.

"Um…we were just heading up to my room. Did you need something?"

"Oh, no. You guys go ahead. I was checking to see if you

were home yet. I was working on something." He waved the papers around, "and lost track of time."

I turned to Eli, who stood waiting quietly during the exchange. "You ready?"

"As ever." He smiled.

"Okay, guess we can go up." I walked over to my dad and kissed him on the cheek. "See you later."

As I walked toward the stairs, I felt Eli's eyes on me. It was kind of unnerving, yet also thrilling.

The past couple of days had certainly been a rollercoaster. Now, to just keep myself from falling out of the cart. I could do this. We would talk, and things would be okay.

Chapter Twenty-Eight

Eli

When we walked into Emma's room, I immediately noticed the pink rose sitting on top of her dresser. I stared a second, but didn't say a word. For once Em broke her parent's "door stays open" rule. I got the feeling it wasn't for anything her parents had to be worried about.

Instead of sitting on the bed like usual, we both gravitated toward the floor. I leaned against the wall next to an old guitar Emma had bought years ago, then never learned how to play, and couldn't help but smile a little remembering how she complained that it gave her callouses. She sat cross-legged near me.

I picked at a frayed shoelace, trying to think how to start. "Why'd you do it?" I couldn't look at her when I asked the question.

I felt her shift, her body rocking side to side slightly. "I guess…I guess because I wasn't brave enough to tell you to your face."

My hand stilled on the shoelace. "Tell me what?" Would she finally admit it? I needed for her to say the words. I felt like so much of it had been a game, and I needed to know where I stood.

"Eli, look…I owe you an apology for what I did, and I realize that. I shouldn't have pretended to be someone I wasn't to talk to you. And I shouldn't have kept it going as long as I did."

"You said you were going to tell me why you went out with him."

We were back to the obvious elephant in the room. *Jake.*

"At first I did it because of you going out with Kelli."

I stared at her, sure I hadn't heard her correctly.

"But there was no Kelli. It was you, so that doesn't even make sense."

She sighed. "I know it was me, but you were going on about asking her out and I didn't know what to say."

My eyes felt like they were about to pop out of my head. "So you decided to go out with some guy you don't even know because I was telling you that I was going to ask you out?" I shook my head. "Do you realize how stupid that sounds?"

"No, it doesn't sound stupid to me, because I didn't know it was me you were going to ask out. I thought it was her."

"And how the hell could I ask *her* out? She doesn't even exist."

"Well I didn't know that!" Emma began to yell too.

My mouth gaped open. "Of course you did! You're the one who made her up!"

She jumped to her feet. "I know that!"

I stood as well, hands on my hips. "Are you insane? You just said you thought I was going to ask out a fictional girl, so that's why you went out with him."

"I know what I said. And it's the truth."

She'd completely lost it. I covered my face for a moment.

"So, let me get this straight," I said slowly. "You make up some bogus profile and send me a friend request so I'd start talking to you. Oh wait, so I'd start talking to *Kelli*."

I knew my voice dripped sarcasm saying the name, but I couldn't rein it in. "Then, you say all this crap to me about how great you think I am. When I say I'm going to ask you out, to try to see what you think, you instead decide that 'hey, I better go out with someone else.'" My hands clenched at my sides. "I see you with him, acting like the love-struck little couple. Then the next day, I see you with *that*"—I jerked my head toward the rose—"and you see me in the window and you look like you're ready to puke."

She looked at the rose, then back at me. "What? No, you don't understand!"

So maybe jerk didn't send it. "Fine, maybe I jumped the gun there. I know your parents have already done that stuff."

Before she could say anything, I continued. "Then *you* come up to *me* and say you want to talk, only you haven't really said anything at all. Did I get it all about right?"

Emma looked confused.

"Well, yes, but—"

"Yeah, I thought so. So, tell me, what's going on with you and...what's his name again? John? Jackass?"

"Jake," she mumbled.

"Oh yeah, Jake. What's going on with you and *Jake* now?" I practically spit out the words.

She lifted her chin by a fraction. "I'm supposed to be seeing him later."

Her admission knocked me mute. For a minute.

"Well I don't really see what more there is to talk about, do you?"

"Eli, you don't understand." She reached out to touch my arm.

I jerked away. "Oh, I understand. I understand plenty.

I hope you guys have fun tonight." I couldn't believe how dumb I'd been. I'd actually thought we had a chance, that she wanted to be with me. And to hear she had a date with him tonight? I needed to get out of there.

"Don't. Would you just wait?" Her tone was pleading.

"Why? So you can tell me all about him? Thanks, but no thanks."

"Eli, stop it. You never…"

I stopped, whirling around to face her. "I never what? What, Em?"

She shook her head. "Nothing. Never mind."

"Yeah, it clearly doesn't matter anyway." I opened the door, and began to walk through it, pausing again in the archway. "For the record, I did more than you. And at least when I did it, I wasn't faking."

Chapter Twenty-Nine

Emma

How did it all go so wrong? When Eli said everything, it was technically correct, but somehow it didn't sound right when he'd gone through it. It all sounded twisted and distorted. It didn't begin to cover how I'd felt through it all, what I'd meant.

I wanted to apologize, to explain, but part of me wasn't sure what I was really apologizing for. He'd apparently known from almost the get-go, so it wasn't like I'd deceived him. If anything, he deceived me. He'd kept it from me that he knew the truth.

The doubts grew. Why was he doing this? If he meant any of the things he'd said to me as Kelli, why wasn't he saying anything now? Did he actually like me, or did he just want me to say it to him to stroke his ego? But that wasn't him. I told myself to stop thinking crap about Eli. Told myself I knew him better than that.

Sinking to the floor, I couldn't wrap my head around how bad things had gotten. I leaned my head against the wall and closed my eyes, feeling my chest tighten and tears threaten. Again.

What was I supposed to do about seeing Jake tonight? Part of me just wanted to cancel immediately, but a small, hesitant part wondered if the best thing to do was just move on. To accept that things with Eli would simply never be the way I'd always dreamed.

My mind wandered back to Jake. He was great, but right now, with my feelings for Eli so strong, it probably wasn't a good time to start something with anyone else. It wouldn't be fair to him. And even if I told him we could go out just as friends, feeling like this, I wouldn't exactly make great company.

It would definitely make things worse between me and Eli.

I opened my eyes, staring blankly out the window. My gaze eventually shifted to the photos on the bookshelf a few feet away. Things had been so much easier back then. I picked up a paperback from the floor nearby and threw it. Its pages fluttered open as it sailed through the air before bouncing near the shelves and landing with a thud.

Eli obviously made his decision when he walked out. Maybe a night away from dealing with the whole mess was exactly what I needed.

Chapter Thirty

Emma

"Girls' night! Girls' night!" Sarah chanted through the phone. *Emphatically*.

I'd called Sarah as promised to tell her what happened with Eli after school. After hearing the news, Sarah said I should dump all my men for the evening and make it a girls' night instead.

"And who are we inviting to this festive occasion?" I muttered.

"Why don't you call Megan? She's really nice and would probably be fun to have along."

"I haven't had her over in like a year."

"So what? Call her anyway. Or heck, I'll call her." Sarah wasn't taking no for an answer.

"Okay, you ask her. What time do you guys want to come over?" Maybe time alone with the girls would be exactly what I needed. I smiled, remembering how we used to have sleepovers all the time in junior high.

"We'll be there around six. Be ready to head out for a little."

After that abrupt command, the line went silent as Sarah hung up. Now I had to let Jake know that our date for this evening wouldn't be happening. I stared into space for a minute, trying to think of an excuse that wouldn't sound like I was blowing him off. None came to mind, mostly because I *was* sort of blowing him off. Even if it was with the kindest of intentions.

Snatching the phone back up, I scrolled through my contacts until I found his name. I'd take the coward's way out and send him a text breaking the news.

Jake, I'm really sorry, but I need to cancel for tonight. I need to clear my head a little, so I'm just hanging out with Sarah. Maybe another time?

Less than a minute later, I got my response.

That's ok, I kind of expected that. And sure, another time would be good. Have fun tonight.

I wasn't sure what I expected to feel after cancelling, but surprisingly, I only felt a bit relieved.

After checking with my dad to make sure it was okay that Sarah and Megan were sleeping over and to let him know we would probably be going out for dinner, I started getting ready for the night ahead.

Megan was able to come, too. The three of us piled into Sarah's bright orange beat-up VW Bug, headed to grab something to eat. As usual, Sarah looked adorable in a stretchy long black skirt and an iridescent peasant blouse. She could throw on aluminum cans and still look fashionable. Megan dressed more like I usually did, in jeans and a pink T-shirt.

I'd decided to try to add a little variety to my outfit. Although jeans were still on the menu, I had pulled out a shirt Sarah bought me last year. I'd only worn it once, thinking it was a little too much for me. It was a silvery white loose halter with a low-scooped back. But since tonight was all about relaxing and having fun, I decided to go for it.

Sarah had the radio blasting, so when Kelly Clarkson's "People Like Us" came on, all three of us screamed and began to sing along at the top of our lungs. I rolled my window down even further, loving the feel of the wind whipping through my hair as the music washed over me.

It felt so good to relax and not worry about anything. I smiled when Sarah pumped her fist in the air out her window and sang along full throttle.

"So throw your fists in the air, come out, come out if you dare, tonight we're gonna change forever!"

"Amen!" yelled Megan. "Sing it!"

I laughed and moved my head in time to the beat as Sarah pulled into a coveted front parking space at Roma.

"See girls? Tonight is our night. We don't even have to hike to get to the front door." Sarah winked and shifted into park.

The lot was almost completely full already. Groups of families and packs of teenagers walked in and out of the front doors.

"It's pretty crowded for a Tuesday," Megan said.

"Probably since school's out for break. Hopefully we can get a seat." I jumped out after Sarah and Megan, glancing around to see if there were any recognizable cars in the lot. Namely, Eli or Jake's. It didn't look like either one of them were there, although I didn't really expect them to be.

The warm air smelled of fresh baked bread and spicy Italian sauces. Hints of pink streaked through the clouds. The perfect setting for hanging with friends.

My stomach growled as we headed toward the door, and I held my hand over it, laughing. "I didn't realize how hungry I am."

"I'm starving," Sarah agreed, pulling open the glass door.

Crowds of people packed around a small bar, and the tables up front were all full. The aroma of food became even more prominent the moment we stepped inside.

"Maybe there's a booth open in the back?" Megan asked, as we stood just inside the door, looking around, eyes wide.

"Holy shit, I don't remember ever seeing it this busy. We seriously did luck out finding a parking space." Sarah pushed through the small line of people waiting to use the restroom. Her tiny frame didn't stop her from being a formidable force.

"What the heck? Is something going on in town? This is nuts." I followed the path Sarah made. We zig-zagged toward the larger back room that contained booths on one end and arcade games in the far back.

"Hey! There's one!" Megan waved her arm in the air and pointed wildly. "Hurry, let's get it before someone else does." She weaved over to the right, where an empty booth sat with a couple of glasses and a half-empty pitcher of soda.

"Oh, good call, Meg." Sarah congratulated her. "Looks like they just didn't get a chance to clear it yet."

If possible, this room had even less free space than the front, with crowds of people playing the video games and using the pool or air hockey tables in the back.

"Finally." I slid into the slightly sticky booth. My hand stuck to something on the table. "Ew."

"Here." Sarah handed me a napkin from the table dispenser. "I'm sure someone will be by to clear it off soon."

"Thanks." I wiped my fingers, wrinkling my nose when the paper stuck a little.

"So what do we want?" Megan asked. "Pizza? Wings?"

"Hmm…why not go crazy and have both?" I suggested with a grin.

"Works for me," Sarah said, craning her neck trying to spot a server so we could place an order. Suddenly, she whipped her head back around, a look of shock clear on her face. "Emma, don't look now."

"What?" I began to turn to look too.

"Emma!" Sarah kicked me under the table. "I said don't look. Just…here." She shoved a large menu toward me. "Cover your face with this."

"What? Why?" I tried to skim the room without being obvious, peeking over the top of the red plastic menu.

Oh please, no. Eli and Kevin were headed our way. I sank down further in my seat, trying desperately to make myself disappear.

Invisibility was apparently not my hidden superpower, because moments later, the two guys stopped right next to our table.

Kevin slid into the booth next to Sarah. "Hey, sexy, keeping the seat warm for me?" He winked.

Sarah rolled her eyes and shifted farther against the wall in an attempt to make some space between them. "Get lost."

Eli simply stood next to the booth, looking completely uncomfortable with the entire situation. He didn't say a word, and refused to even glance my way.

Megan, oblivious to the situation unfolding, jumped into friendly mode. "Hey guys, it's packed, but we can slide in so we can all fit. Come on, we don't mind." She smiled and pushed closer to the wall, motioning for me to slide over as well to make room for Eli.

I didn't know what to do. It wasn't like I could explain the awkwardness of the situation with Eli standing only inches away, and Kevin leaning across the table smirking.

"Actually, ladies, you're in *our* seats." Kevin leaned back and crossed his arms across his chest. "But hey, I'm a giving man." Another sleazy wink. "I'm willing to share with the three of you."

"What are you talking about? We were here first." Sarah elbowed him in the ribs, hard. "You're lucky I'm not shoving your ass on the floor."

"No, we were here first." Eli finally spoke up, quietly. He motioned to the glasses on the table. "They're ours. We already ordered, and just went back to play a few games until our food got here."

"Oh. Sorry about that," little miss sunshine Megan bubbled. "Well, do you guys mind if we sit here too?"

"No, we'll find another table." I stood up, attempting to slip past Eli, and motioned for the other girls to follow. Megan looked confused, while Sarah appeared resigned. Eli didn't protest our leaving, but he also didn't move out of my way.

I held my hands out, looking at the other girls. "Well? Are we finding somewhere else to sit?"

Sarah shook her head. "Emma, look around. There aren't any other empty tables. I'm hungry, and I just want to eat."

I couldn't believe what I was hearing. Sarah knew this wasn't a good idea. I stared at her, gaze pointed, before looking to Megan for support.

"We might as well all stay here," Megan said. "If they don't mind, that is," she hastily added.

"Oh no, I don't mind at all." Kevin chortled. "Hey, Eli, do you mind?" He obviously knew some of the backstory to be that amused.

Eli shot him a look, then seemed to realize his silence made him appear rude. "No. I don't mind. Just stay, no big deal." He motioned for me to sit back down.

Megan sighed happily to have it all resolved.

I wanted to go in the bathroom and throw up.

Clearly having no choice in the matter short of walking

out of the restaurant by myself, I sat back down. Since Kevin didn't seem inclined to move over on his side of the booth, I slid closer to Megan, making room for Eli. He finally took a seat next to me.

The booth normally seated two people on each side, so the three of us pressed tight against each other. Despite trying to sit as far away as possible without falling out, Eli's leg was in direct contact with mine. Each of his movements allowed me to feel the shift in his thigh muscles, wreaking havoc with my ability to concentrate on any conversation going on around me.

Completely oblivious, Megan leaned across me to ask Eli questions about some project for school. Rather than be rude and talk to the side of my head, Eli also leaned forward, which caused him to encroach even more on my personal space. His breath warmed my check and neck as he answered Megan.

I closed my eyes and willed myself to relax.

"You okay over there, Emma?" Kevin's annoying voice broke my self-pep talk.

Embarrassed, I opened my eyes and smiled with saccharine sweetness. "I'm just fine. Thanks for asking." I wanted to knock his teeth down his throat.

Trying to shift in my seat to look for the server proved difficult while squashed between two other people. "How long ago did you guys order?"

"About thirty minutes or so. It should be here soon." Eli spoke directly to me for the first time since we sat down.

On cue, the harried server arrived at our table balancing a large pizza on a metal serving tray in one hand and two plates in the other.

"Oh!" she exclaimed, looking at our group at the table. "Do you need more plates?" She slid the pie onto the table, and set the plates next to it with an inquiring look.

"No," Sarah said. "We'd like to place a separate order if

that's okay."

While Sarah placed the order, the rest of us sat awkwardly, not saying a word.

Eli broke the silence. "It's crazy in here. I heard there was some art and music exhibit at the middle school, so I'm guessing a lot of families stopped in after that." He reached out to grab a slice and slid it onto his empty plate. Kevin did the same. "Do you guys want a piece until yours gets here?" Eli asked.

"No, I'm good. I'll wait for ours, thanks." Sarah and Megan also waved off his offer, thanking him.

He shrugged and took a large bite.

Silence fell on the table as they began to eat.

I wiggled my foot under the table, trying to think of something to say. The side of my foot smacked into a muscled shin. "Sorry," I muttered in Eli's direction.

His smile was tense. "No problem."

Everyone else at the table looked at us.

"I kicked him. Well, not on purpose obviously, because why would I do that?" I closed my mouth before I could sound any more like a babbling idiot. My nerves were definitely getting the best of me.

Eli cleared his throat, while Kevin snorted.

"Okay, well, why don't we play a game while we wait?" Megan suggested.

"It's packed back there, and I don't want to waste any more money," Kevin said. "Besides, I'm hungry and I don't want the pizza to get cold."

"No, I mean here. At the table." She clapped. "Oh, I know one!"

Sarah rolled her eyes, but laughed. "Sure, I'm in."

"Okay. It's called 'would you rather,' and each of us takes turns picking someone that has to answer a question. And you have to be honest," Megan explained.

Kevin made a "let's go" motion with his hand, before shoveling a huge bite of pizza in his mouth. "We got it, get on with it," he instructed, mouth full.

"I'll go first." Megan paused, looking around the table at each of us. "Sarah."

"Yes?"

"Would you rather eat a live spider or jump in a pit of snakes?" Megan giggled.

"Gross. Neither."

"You have to pick one. That's the rule," she said.

"Okay, fine. I guess jump in a pit of snakes. But I get to wear some super-padded outfit so I don't have to feel them, and I'm getting back out right away."

Everyone laughed.

"So now what?" Kevin asked, reaching for his second slice.

"Now Sarah gets to pick someone and ask a question."

Sarah glanced around the table. Meanwhile, the server came back with our cups and the other pitcher of soda. Eli thanked her and began to pour one for each of us, passing them down the table.

"I pick Kevin," Sarah said, a wicked smile on her face.

"Of course you do, babe." He waggled his eyebrows.

"Oh shut up. I'd eat the spider before that."

Everyone but Kevin cracked up. Instead, he slung an arm around Sarah's shoulders and leaned in making kissing noises.

"Oh, gross. Get off me you Neanderthal." Sarah smacked his arm away. "Anyway, would you rather make out with Sam or Dean from Supernatural?" She smiled triumphantly.

"What the hell kind of question is that?"

"It's my question, and you have to choose. That's the rule." She pointed at Megan. "She said so."

"I don't care if that's the rule. That question is freaking moronic. I don't pick either."

I laughed watching him sputter. "You have to answer, Kevin."

"Oh for…fine. You pick one. It's stupid anyway." He shot me a glare.

"I can't answer for you, it's not my question."

"Whatever. Dean. Though it's dumb because everyone knows I don't swing that way." He grabbed his glass and took a long drink, glaring.

I laughed.

"Fine, Emma. I pick *you* for my question."

I shouldn't have pissed him off. "Okay, go. Ask away," I said in a breezy tone. This wasn't going to be good, I could tell. My lips pressed together in a fake smile, and I shrugged nonchalantly.

He smiled back. An evil smile. "So tell us, would you rather"—he paused for effect before continuing—"kiss Eli"—he pointed his slice in Eli's direction—"or your boy, Jake?"

The blood drained from my face.

Eli placed his slice back down on his plate, jaw clenched.

Kevin smirked.

Sarah looked aghast, while Megan just giggled a little before asking, "Who's Jake?"

"Yeah, Emma, why don't you tell us all about him?" Kevin asked.

Punching his teeth down his throat wasn't good enough. I wanted to grab the serving knife and stab it through his black little heart.

"That's a stupid question. Give me another."

Eli turned to stare at me. His eyes were unreadable. "Why can't you answer?"

"It's not that I can't answer. No one else got a question like that."

"What are you talking about? She asked me about kissing

two dudes!" Kevin argued.

"That's different."

"You have to answer!" Megan piped in.

Eli still watched me, jaw twitching. No matter what I said, it wouldn't be the right answer. If I said Eli, I'd look like a fool since he'd made it clear he was mad at me, and barely even wanted to speak to me. If I said Jake, well, there was no way that would go over well either.

"We're waiting," Kevin said. "Tick, tock."

I took a sip of my soda, stalling for time. *Who would I rather kiss?* The image that popped in my head was as clear as day, the answer to the question, the only real answer there could be, if I was honest with myself.

Swallowing, I lowered my head, whispering, "Eli. I'd rather kiss Eli."

A sharp intake of breath sounded to my left. Ignoring the catcalls around me, I peeked Eli's way, trying to gauge his reaction to my response.

He looked right at me. This time, his eyes showed relief. And something else. Something I was almost afraid to identify. *Desire.*

Chapter Thirty-One

Emma

Everything else faded in that moment. Acutely aware of how each point our bodies touched on the crowded seat, it became increasingly difficult to not scream, "*Would you just kiss me already?*"

Eli's eyes changed from their mix of blues and greens to a smoky gray. He was magic. A touch on my hand sent shivers through my body. *Eli's touch.*

Something pegged off the side of my head breaking the trance. I blinked, reaching up to see what hit me. I pulled a wadded-up straw wrapper out of my hair where it had stuck in one of my curls.

"Get a room," Kevin muttered. He didn't look thrilled that his little plan didn't work the way he'd expected. Apparently, he'd been looking forward to a scene of Eli and me fighting, not making ga-ga faces at each other.

Eli pulled his hand away, shifting on the seat. He cleared his throat, and his neck flushed slightly. Sarah, on the other hand, looked very interested in what just happened on the other side of the booth.

What *had* happened? The look in his eyes, had I imagined it? No. It was there. He'd wanted to kiss me, too.

"Oh, here comes our food, finally!" Megan was ever oblivious, or else she didn't care about the soap opera going down right next to her.

I stole another quick glance at Eli, and we shared a private smile before we turned our attention back to what was going on around us.

The server headed toward our table, carrying the pizza and wings. We all attempted to clear some room on the table for her to set the food down.

"Here you go, sorry about the wait. It's a little backed up tonight." She brushed her forehead with the back of her hand. "Can I get you anything else?"

"No we're good, thanks."

Sarah took charge of our meal, divvying up the wings on small plates and handing them out. Kevin reached out and grabbed one out of the basket.

"Oh, by all means, help yourself," Sarah said.

"Thanks, I will." He shoved the whole thing in his mouth.

"You know, it really is such a shocker that you don't have a girlfriend." I wrinkled my nose as he sucked the last of the sauce noisily.

"Hey, we can't all string two people along like you do, Emma."

"Knock it off, Kevin." Eli said, shooting Kevin a death stare.

"What? I'm only stating the obvious."

"Give it a rest." Eli's tone held warning.

"Whatever, man." Kevin leaned back in the booth, crossing his arms in front of him.

He'd stuck up for me. Trying not to smile, I reached for my slice and took a bite. The tangy sauce tasted delicious. Or, maybe the idea of Eli standing up for me and seeming to want to kiss me made it taste so good.

We finished the meal without any more drama, keeping the conversation to general topics. The awkward moment of 'what now' came after the food was gone. We hadn't arrived together, but I really wished Eli and I could spend some alone time after the moment we shared.

Sarah had other ideas. "Okay, ladies, time to commence girls' night." She clapped her hands briskly. "Gentleman, it's been a pleasure, but we're outta here."

I felt Eli's gaze. Looking over, I gave a tiny shrug. It wouldn't be right to bail on Megan and Sarah. He seemed to understand, and offered a small smile before standing up to allow us room to slide out of the booth.

"Wait, we don't have our check yet." I scanned the booth.

We all looked around for our server, but she was nowhere to be seen.

"Super," muttered Sarah. "This will take forever."

"Why don't you guys go? I'll take care of it when she brings it." Eli shrugged. "I'm not in a hurry to get anywhere."

"Great, thanks!" Sarah immediately replied, pushing Kevin to move so she could get out too.

"Here, we'll give you the money." I reached into my bag and pulled a ten-dollar bill from my wallet. Sarah and Megan each did the same, handing it to Eli.

"Well, I guess we're going," I said, not sure what else to say.

He seemed equally at a loss for words, shuffling his feet and tapping on the tabletop. He nodded, looking right at me. "Have fun."

I smiled. "We will."

"Come on," Sarah called, bored with the goodbyes and starting to walk away.

"I guess you better go," he said softly.

"Yeah. See ya later."

"Bye."

I turned to walk away, but only got three steps before he stopped me, his hand on my arm.

"I'll call you tomorrow, okay?"

"That'd be great." I beamed.

"Cool." His face lit up in a wide smile, just for me. "Well, okay. I'll talk to you then." He brushed his fingers down my arm all the way to my hand, which he squeezed before letting go.

My heart rate doubled timed.

"Talk to you then."

"Oh my God, can we *go* already?" Sarah tapped her watch and gave me a pointed look.

I laughed. "I'm coming." Walking away, my heart soared. It was really happening. I couldn't believe it.

As we walked through the parking lot to Sarah's car, Megan looked my way. "So what's going on with you and Eli anyway?"

"No. No, no, *no*! We are not talking boys tonight, especially not *that* saga," Sarah said, shaking her head emphatically. "Tonight is a night for manicures, makeovers, junk food, and movies." She unlocked the car. "That's it." She laughed.

The three of us climbed into the small car to head back to my house.

"Sounds like a plan," I agreed, smiling at both of them.

On the drive home, we chatted about whether or not we wanted French tips or solid colors, if we should try straightening my hair to see what it looked like, and what kind of candy we wanted to buy. Simple topics. Welcome topics.

A block before the grocery store where we planned to stop to buy our chocolate fix, my phone beeped. Eli. Warmth rushed through me just seeing his name displayed.

I wish I had just kissed you like I wanted to.

My pulse sped up reading his admission. He'd wanted to kiss me, and he was thinking about it *right now*. I glanced up at the front seat, where Sarah and Megan discussed what we should get at the store.

Lowering the phone so they couldn't see what I was doing, I took a deep breath and typed,

Me too.

It felt funny being able to tell him that, finally. I waited impatiently to see if he'd say anything else. His response was quick.

:)

I grinned and bit my lip. It was a heady sensation—Eli thinking about wanting to kiss me.

Lights washed over the car. We'd arrived at the store. Megan and Sarah turned around to face me.

"Oh no," Sarah groaned.

"What?"

"You've got that face on."

I looked back and forth from Sarah to Megan. "What are you talking about? What face?"

Megan giggled and nodded at Sarah.

"What face?" I repeated.

"The *I have Eli on the brain* face," Sarah said.

I snorted. "I do not."

"Yep, you do," Megan agreed, nodding again.

"Oh shut up." I laughed, reaching for the door handle.

"Nope, you can't go in with us."

"What are you talking about, why not?"

"Because," Sarah stretched out the word, "You will be absolutely useless as a member of the girls-only club tonight." She raised one brow.

I stared at her. "What do you mean? Snickers, M&Ms, Tootsie Rolls, let's go get them."

"Emma, you've been in love with Eli most of your life."

I opened my mouth, but Sarah held up a hand, stopping me from interrupting.

"It's a fact. I know it and you know it." She looked over at Megan, "And well, now she knows it too." Megan tipped her head.

"And after the little display earlier, which by the way, came very close to needing an R-rating based on sexual tension alone"—she raised her eyebrows—"I don't really think we're the company you want tonight, though it was very nice of you to pretend otherwise."

"Stop it. Of course I want to hang out with you."

Sarah and Megan looked at each other, then both shook their heads and laughed. "Yeah, right. Anyway, consider this an 'I owe you.'" Sarah smiled. "Em, I'm happy for you. Seriously. And what kind of friend would I be if I kept you from what you've waited for this long?"

A smile began to creep over my face and I bit my lip to try to hold it back.

"I saw you texting, and I have a pretty good idea who you're talking to." Sarah grinned. "For goodness sake, call him and tell him you want to see him tonight."

I looked at both of my friends, trying to decide if they really meant it. I squealed. "Are you sure? I can't help it, I just—"

"We know. And we're sure." Sarah pointed at me. "But this is a one-time only offer. We still stand by our hos over bros motto any other night." She winked. "And I definitely want details later, got it?"

"Got it." My huge grin broke through. I had the best friends in the world.

Sarah looked to Megan, "Well, looks like it's just you and me tonight. We can go back to my house. After we get chocolate." They laughed. "We'll be in the store so you can call Prince Charming in private." She made kissy noises before climbing out, still laughing.

I waited until they entered the store to dial Eli's number.

As it rang, I suddenly got nervous. What was I supposed to say? What if he didn't want to hang out tonight? Was I being too pushy?

"Hello?" His voice washed over me like a warm summer rain.

I smiled into the phone. "Hey, it's me."

He laughed. "I know. What's up? I thought you were hanging out with Sarah and Megan."

I played with the strap of my bag. "I am. I was. I'm not anymore." Oh geez, I couldn't even complete a full sentence. Holding my breath, I waited to hear his response.

"Oh!" When he spoke again, his voice was warm, teasing. "So does this mean you're now free tonight?"

I blushed and smiled like a little kid. Thank goodness he couldn't see me. "Yes."

"Well in that case…" The smile in his voice came through loud and clear. "Do you want to do something? With me?" He stumbled over the last words. He was so cute.

I beamed again. "I'd really like that."

"We're almost home. Kevin drove, so how about I come over for you as soon as I get back? Is that okay?"

"Sounds good. I'll be home soon, too. We stopped at the store to grab a couple things, Sarah and Megan are inside."

"Okay, I'll see you soon."

"See you soon."

"And Em? I'm *really* glad you called."

"Me, too." I paused. "Bye."

"See you soon," he repeated.

I disconnected the call, unable to stop the huge grin from spreading across my face. It was really, really happening. I was going out on a date…*with Eli.* I wanted to cheer aloud, settling instead for a little dance in the backseat. I couldn't wait to see him again.

Chapter Thirty-Two

Eli

"So what was that all about?" Kevin shot me a look as he swung into my driveway.

I kind of regretted letting him drive in the first place. I'd listened to him grill me the entire ride home, and now that he heard the phone call, well, he obviously put two and two together.

"Dude, drop it." I got that he thought he was looking out for me, but Kevin didn't know Emma the way I did. He was convinced all females were out to use men and then drop us when they were through. Pretty hypocritical considering how he treated women. Then again, considering that his mom took off without a word when he was eight, I kind of understood why he was so jaded.

"Look, all I'm saying is— "

"I know what you're saying. I get it, and I appreciate it. But this is something I have to do. Something I *want* to do." I opened the car door and stepped out. I leaned down. "I get it man, but you've got to understand, Emma's important to me. You've gotta respect that."

He nodded. "I hope it works for you, bro."

I shut the door and slapped his roof twice. "You and me both."

She'd be home soon. I went in the house and called out, "I'm going over to Emma's for a while." Television sounded from the den. I didn't wait for a response from my parents, they'd figure out where I was.

Taking the stairs two at a time, I ran up to the bathroom to brush my teeth. If there was any chance of actually kissing Emma tonight, it was *not* going to be with me having garlic and black olive breath. After rinsing with some mouthwash for good measure, I breathed into my palm. Good to go.

I grabbed a clean shirt and ripped the old one off. It felt kind of strange going through all of these motions to go to Emma's. We'd seen each other sick with the flu, walking around in PJs when we were younger, and here I was primping like a girl. Dumb or not, I wanted her to think I looked nice. I swiped some deodorant on; hopefully she'd think I smelled okay too.

After running my fingers through my hair and staring at myself in the mirror a few seconds, I took a deep breath. Show time. I couldn't help but break into a grin.

I crossed the yard to her house, and walked in. When I reached her bedroom, I gave my usual three-tap knock and opened the door.

And immediately froze.

All breath left my body. My heart may have stopped for a second, I'm not quite sure.

Emma stood about five feet away, arms up over her head tangled in some kind of shirt. But the shirt above her head wasn't what held my attention. The fact that she was only wearing a bra with her jeans was what stopped me in my tracks.

You'd think for all the times I'd had my arm around her, or that we'd wrestled, I would have had a better idea what she had going on under her shirts. Because…*wow*. My mouth went dry and I couldn't form a word. My eyes probably looked like those oversized kinds you see in cartoons.

Emma was…a knockout. Just the right amount of curves. The bra suited her, some pale pink thing with hints of lace that made me wonder what secrets it was hiding.

"Eli!" Her shocked scream broke me out of my trance, and her face turned a vivid shade of red.

She quickly crossed both arms over her chest, like that would help considering I'd already gotten a pretty good peek.

Her eyes were saucers.

My mouth opened and closed several times, but nothing came out.

"What…what are you doing here?" She seemed afraid to uncross her arms to pull the shirt on, like that might give me another free display.

It wasn't like I'd tried to walk in on her getting dressed. I wasn't some perv.

"I…I told you I was coming over," I said defensively, and swallowed down the egg in my throat. "I'm sorry. I didn't know you were changing."

"Well, I am." She blinked rapidly.

"Yeah, I see that." My mouth twitched. I couldn't help but start to see the humor in the situation.

Clearly, she hadn't reached that point yet.

"Um…so do you mind? I'd like to finish getting dressed." She was so cute when she blushed.

I took a step into the room. "By all means, don't stop on my account." I couldn't resist teasing her. The twitching turned into a full-fledged grin.

"Eli!"

"Fine, I'll turn around."

"Would you just leave the room a minute?"

I spun away, facing the half-closed door. "I promise I won't peek. Go ahead." I so wanted to peek. I couldn't get the image of her in that pink scrap of next to nothing out of my mind. But I kept my word.

Seconds later, she said, "You can turn around now."

I turned back to face her, but before I could say anything, Emma held up a hand. "Don't. Just don't." Her cheeks still matched the bra I knew she wore under the T-shirt. I fought back a grin.

"What? I wasn't going to say a word!" I feigned innocence.

"Right." She tugged at the hem of her shirt. "So, did you want to hang out here or go do something, or what?"

She was clearly embarrassed, so I decided to let her off the hook. For now. "Do you want to walk down to the Freeze and get some ice cream? Then we can come back here and watch a movie if you want." I shrugged. "I figured it's nice out and it's still early."

She nodded and forced an awkward smile. "That sounds like fun. Too bad miniature golf is still closed. I could kick your butt at that!"

I snorted. "Dream on."

The image of her when I walked in still danced in my mind. Emma wasn't fake beautiful, she was breathtaking in her own natural way. And she had absolutely no idea what she did to me.

I crossed the few steps to where she stood, and reached out to poke around her middle where I knew she was most ticklish. She swatted me away, laughing. "Knock it off, Eli. I mean it!"

But touching her, even teasing, felt too good. I stood behind her, wrapping my arms around her, running my fingers down her sides tickling her even more. Her hair smelled like strawberries and springtime rolled together. I wanted to do so much more than just tickle her, but it wasn't the right time. Not yet.

I leaned in to whisper, "So, was that the bra you told me you were shopping for that night?" and snickered.

She jabbed me in the ribs. "Oh shut up."

I laughed and released my hold. Emma made a show of striding over to the door with her chin raised, ignoring me, so I caught up and whispered again, "By the way, it was a nice choice, I liked it."

She spun around. "Okay fine, so you saw me in my bra. You liked my choice. I got it, can we go now?" Her voice had risen.

I cleared my throat, trying to swallow.

"What?" she asked. "Not so funny now?" Her grin was teasing.

"I believe he's trying to figure out a way to tell you that I'm standing behind you."

Emma paled. After a heartbeat, she slowly turned to face her father, who stood just outside her partially opened door with his arms crossed and eyebrows raised.

"Dad! I…we…um…"

Her dad heard the whole bra comment. Things *so* didn't look good. I stepped forward quickly, pulling the door open all the way and stammering, "Sir, it isn't what it sounded like. Trust me." I held up my hand like I was a boy scout, or taking an oath.

Her father raised his eyebrows even further.

"Dad, it was an accident. I didn't realize he was coming over so soon, and I got toothpaste all over my shirt so I had to change, and then he walked in as I was putting my shirt on, that's all, I swear." Emma seemed to run out of breath trying to get the explanation out in one long sentence.

I was more interested in the fact that she'd been concerned about brushing her teeth, too.

Her dad pressed his lips together, but I swore he was also fighting back a laugh. "Well, I'd suggest you make sure to *lock* your door next time you're getting dressed," he finally said. "That way we won't have something like this happen again." He stared at us in turn. "Understood?"

"Yes."

"Yes, sir." I nodded my head up and down emphatically. I wanted to crawl in a hole.

"All right, then."

An uncomfortable silence ensued as we all tried to figure out what to say or do next. Her dad looked around the bedroom. "I thought your friends were staying over tonight?"

"They were, but there was…ah…a change in plans." Emma smiled weakly.

The eyebrows went up again.

"We were headed out to the Freeze. Is that still okay?"

Mr. Kurtz looked at me for a long second, head cocked, before nodding slowly. "That's fine." He turned his gaze on Emma. "I want you home by ten. That still gives you"—he checked his watch—"almost two hours, which should be plenty of time to go for ice cream."

I shuffled my feet, looking down, still feeling awkward with the entire situation.

As we stepped through the door, her dad moved out of the way to allow us to pass. "Oh, and kids?"

We both turned.

"Have fun." He smiled, reaching out and ruffling Emma's hair.

The breath *whooshed* out when I realized he believed us and wasn't ticked, or banning me from their home.

"We will, thanks, Dad." Emma smiled.

"Now get out of here." He waved us off.

We made our way out of the house as quickly as we could. Once the front door closed behind us, I covered my face with my hand. "I will never be able to look your father in the eyes again, so help me God."

She laughed and poked me. "Oh stop it. He's fine. He knows it was an accident."

"Yeah, but he's a guy. He might be an old guy, but still. He knows that getting to see someone you like in a bra is never a bad thing." My ears turned warm and I cleared my throat. "Ah…anyway…"

"Why don't we just start over?" She smiled. "Thanks for asking me to go tonight."

I grinned. "My pleasure."

Chapter Thirty-Three

Emma

I'd taken these exact same steps a thousand times with Eli next to me, but it felt totally different right then. The air around us turned electric.

We continued walking along the quiet street. Twilight turned the sky a gorgeous reddish-blue, although storm clouds were beginning to roll in overhead.

"Do you think we should have taken my car? It looks like it's going to rain."

I glanced up. "It's not that far. Hopefully we'll be okay."

The playground came into view to our left. The swings moved slightly, as if ghost children played quietly. Smiling wistfully, I said, "I used to love those as a kid."

"I remember." He reached out for my hand, pulling me in that direction. "Come on."

Stumbling a little, I ran with him, laughing. "Eli! What are you doing?"

"Giving you a ride on the swings. Do you remember how

we'd play on these and have contests to see who could go up the highest?"

"Yes, and you always won. I was too chicken to go that high."

We stepped around the teeter-totter to get to the large metal swing-set. Our footsteps made light cracking noises as we stepped on the wood shavings covering the ground.

"Here, sit down," he said.

I obliged, feeling a little silly, but still loving it.

Grasping the thick steel chains on either side of me, I began to pump my legs to get going. "Aren't you going to swing, too?"

He moved to stand behind me. "Nope. I'm gonna push you." Instead of placing his hands on my back, he reached down and gripped both sides of my waist. Shocks tingled through my body at his unexpected touch. When he leaned in, his breath wove through my hair as he whispered, "Hold on."

Suddenly, he was pulling me back toward him. When he released, I leaned back, looking up at the heavy clouds. He pushed me several more times, laughing at my shrieks and squeals.

After about five minutes, when I leaned back, slightly out of breath, fat raindrops slowly plopped on my face. "Oh no, it's starting to rain."

Eli tilted his head back. "Maybe it's just a shower and it'll blow right over. We're fine." He helped me slow down, and we headed over to the merry-go-round.

Sitting down, we used our feet to make it spin lazily as we sat hip to hip on the old wooden structure. Small puffs of dust appeared around our ankles as we moved in slow, wide circles.

He lightly tapped my toes with his sneaker. I did the same back to him, smiling.

Breathing in the rain-kissed air, the light in the sky dusky and mysterious, the feel of Eli so close…now I knew what heaven felt like. I leaned back, lying flat on the ride, my feet dangling off the edge.

Eli lay back too, joining me. Soft raindrops fell on my forehead and cheeks as I looked up into the darkening sky. The moon played peekaboo with the storm clouds.

"That was fun," I whispered.

"Yeah, it was," he whispered back. After a heartbeat, he reached over and took my hand where it lay between us. His fingers interlaced with mine. Tingles shot through my hand and traveled up my arm. I half expected sparks to shoot between our fingers. We didn't feel a need to even speak for several minutes we simply shared the silence.

"I'm sorry I did all of that," I whispered, turning to look at him.

He faced me, his eyes inches away. They looked deep green in the falling darkness, with flecks of gold showing. He shook his head slightly. "I'm not. I'm glad you did." He squeezed my hand gently. "I was stupid. You were always there, and somehow, I needed that push to really see what I had right in front of me all along." His thumb traced patterns on my hand and he smiled gently. "So please don't be sorry."

I smiled back. We fell silent again, just looking at each other, not needing words.

The light raindrops grew heavier, falling with quick, heavy plops. I squinted, trying to look up, but the rain falling in my eyes made it impossible. A quick clap of thunder, and the clouds broke open in earnest.

"Ah!" I yelled, attempting to cover my head with my arms as I sat up.

Eli stood, reaching to help me up, his dark hair already plastered to his head and face. "Come on," he called, yelling slightly so I could hear him over the sudden downpour.

His wet shirt clung to his chest and shoulders like a second skin. "Em! Come on!" he repeated.

I shook my head, trying not to stare at him standing there all wet and completely gorgeous. I took his offered hand and allowed him to pull me up. Any attempts to block the rain from soaking me by holding an arm over the top of my head were ineffective. Ribbons of water slid down my chest from the long curls sticking to my face and neck.

It was his turn to stare at me.

"What's wrong?" I yelled over a *crack* of lightning.

He didn't answer.

"Eli? What is—"

He stepped forward in one swift movement, his hands cupping my face as he leaned in, his mouth capturing mine.

Time stopped.

Then fireworks exploded everywhere through my body as I stood there completely mesmerized. I finally reacted.

His lips moved even more thoroughly on mine, and his body pressed tighter against me until I wasn't sure where I ended and he began.

I gave in to the moment. He deepened the kiss, exploring my mouth, while his one hand moved to the back of my head, fingers caught in my curls. He tasted like cinnamon and rain. My fantasies hadn't even come close to the reality of kissing Eli.

After what seemed like forever, and yet not nearly long enough, he pulled back slowly. His eyes never left mine, and he stared at me in wonder. Rain flattened his hair, and glistened on his eyelashes. I swallowed, hoping I did it right. There wasn't a doubt in my mind that *he* sure as heck had.

He leaned in once more, his lips softly touching mine, brushing my cheek with the pad of his thumb. My knees buckled slightly. Reaching out to steady myself, I grabbed his shoulder, and then wrapped both of my arms around his neck, holding on. He was the only thing I was aware of. Everything else completely faded away.

I blinked, then tentatively pulled his head closer, needing to feel the pressure of his mouth, wanting to taste him again. My eyes drifted closed as I heard him moan when I touched the tip of my tongue to his full bottom lip and traced it before slipping my tongue inside his waiting mouth.

I pulled back first this time, blinking uncertainly. I bit my lip when he didn't say anything at first. Maybe I *was* doing it wrong.

He ran his hands through my hair on either side of my head, like he didn't want to lose contact with me. "Em," he breathed. He brushed a kiss against my temple, then crushed me against him, holding me tight. He whispered against my ear, "It's always been you."

My heart soared. I closed my eyes, and tried to move in even closer, not wanting the smallest space to separate us. Rain poured down around us, but it didn't matter. I couldn't care less about getting soaked. The boy I fell in love with that long ago summer day was finally holding me in his arms. It was worth the wait.

Chapter Thirty-Four

Emma

We headed back about ten minutes later after realizing the rain wasn't stopping any time soon. Besides, we were both drenched. Of course we'd made good use of our time. I could have kissed Eli forever.

"Sorry we didn't make it to the Freeze," Eli said as we approached my front door, holding hands.

I smiled. "That's okay, I don't mind." *Understatement.*

Pulling the door open, I turned to face him. "We could always watch a movie. We haven't done that in a while."

He wrung the bottom of his shirt out with both hands. "That would be great, but I should really go home and change first."

I giggled. "Yeah, me, too. And it's probably better if you aren't here for it this time."

He held up his hands in mock surrender. "You're right, though I can't say I'd mind."

I blushed, then pushed him off the step. "Go, come on

back when you're done. Except this time, knock on my door *before* you come in."

He jogged toward his house, waving as he went.

I walked in the house. Mom and Dad sat together on the sofa in the living room, both reading. I smiled when I noticed Dad absently stroking my mom's hair.

"I'm home!"

Mom looked up, eyes widening at the sight of me dripping on the landing. "Well hello. I take it you got caught in the rain?"

"Yeah, we did." I couldn't stop my crazy grin.

Her eyes skimmed over me curiously. "Somehow you don't look too upset about that."

Dad lowered his glasses down his nose, watching me now too.

"Oh. Umm…we just had a good time at the playground." I turned red. "We came back when we realized it wasn't stopping."

"I see." Mom's eyes held a knowing glint. "I'm glad you had a nice time, honey."

It didn't take a rocket scientist to figure out that my mom had always suspected how I felt about Eli, and this was her way of saying she was happy for me. A little embarrassed to be so obvious, I excused myself. "I need to go change; Eli's coming over to watch a movie since we didn't get ice cream."

Dad shuffled his newspaper. "Let's make sure there are no more surprise entrances."

Apparently, he hadn't mentioned the incident to Mom, since she looked over at him curiously. He just shook his head. "You don't want to know."

Mom nodded. "Well, have fun. We'll send Eli up when he gets here."

"Thanks." I turned and skipped up the stairs to my room.

As soon as I walked through the door, I saw the rose

sitting on the dresser. Several of the petals had fallen, and scattered around the bud vase. Facts seem to indicate it was from Jake, and there was no way I wanted to start that whole argument again.

Deciding to play it safe, I grabbed the vase and stuck it in the closet on the floor. After swinging the door shut, I walked over to the desk, picked up the fallen petals, and threw them in the trash.

It only took a few minutes to change into a pair of navy yoga pants and a soft, long-sleeved shirt. I was drying my hair with a towel when a familiar knock sounded at my bedroom door. Chuckling to myself, I answered it.

"Don't worry. I'm dressed this time."

Eli laughed and walked into the room. "Damn." He winked.

I pushed him lightly. "Stop it," I warned, giggling.

He peeked out the door, and then leaned in for a quick kiss. Afterward, he smiled at me. "Hey," he said softly.

"Hey back." It seemed surreal. Eli walking in and *kissing* me! "So…" I blushed faintly, curling my toes into the carpet.

He motioned his head over toward the bed. "Why don't we sit down and watch something?"

I followed his motion with my eyes, and my mouth went dry. "Um, why don't we grab some pillows and sit on the floor?"

A grin peeked through. "Sure, that's fine."

Grabbing some of the large pillows from the bed, I settled them on the floor and sat down, facing the television. He chuckled, shaking his head, and joined me. I turned on the TV. "So, what do you want to watch? Are you hungry? Can I get you anything to drink?" I was so nervous.

Eli reached over and took the remote from my hand. "Em."

"What?" My voice shook a little.

He reached to turn my face toward him, gently. "It's me." He shook his head, eyes no longer teasing. "It's me." He brushed the hair back from where it fell into my face.

It's not like we hadn't sat together in my bedroom a million times before, watching TV, talking, listening to music. No matter what else had changed, he was still my best friend in the world.

I nodded. "You're right. I'm sorry. I guess I just..." I shrugged, embarrassed. "It feels different somehow."

"It *is* different. But that's okay. *We're* still the same." He scooted a bit closer. "But, things being kind of different between us isn't a bad thing." He paused. "It's actually a great thing." He looked into my eyes, his expression open and earnest. "For me, anyway."

"It is for me, too," I whispered.

"Okay then. Let's take it as it comes, you know? We don't have to feel all weird around each other, or try to rush anything." He smiled. "We have all the time in the world."

I smiled back. He always knew what to say to make me feel better.

"Deal?" he asked.

"Deal," I echoed.

I stuck out my hand to shake, but he grinned and shook his head. "I have a better idea." He leaned in, slowly, and kissed me. It was feather-soft, and took my breath away.

"I like your way better," I whispered.

He laughed. "Me too."

He left shortly after the movie. I would have been more than happy to sit there all night with him, but I figured Mom and Dad wouldn't be quite so thrilled. Besides, I'd promised the girls I'd give them a call, and knew they'd kill me if I didn't.

So, when he held out his hand to help me up, I accepted with a smile, and offered to walk him downstairs.

"Okay." He smiled, and I had to force myself not to brush his long bangs back from his eyes.

I'd never walked him to the door; any other time he'd always just left on his own. But I kind of hoped he would kiss me again. An official goodnight kiss.

The plan didn't work. My parents were still in the living room, which had a clear view of the front door.

They called goodnight to Eli as we walked past. Mom had that same knowing look, but said nothing. I'm sure she also wondered when Eli got amnesia and forgot how to navigate through our house alone.

"Ah…well, good night," I mumbled, tugging at my shirtsleeve.

He looked quickly into the living room. My parents watched us fumbling around on the landing, clearly enjoying the show, curiosity written all over their faces. How awkward.

"Good night," he said softly, before calling more loudly in my parents' direction, "Good night, Mr. and Mrs. Kurtz."

"Good night, Eli." Dad chuckled into his newspaper.

I rolled my eyes and opened the door. He stepped outside, mouthing, "I'll call you."

Nodding, I smiled and waved before shutting the door.

"I hope with all that you at least got your goodnight kiss before you came down," Dad said dryly, peering over the pages.

I whirled around, cheeks burning.

"Oh, stop teasing the poor girl," my mom scolded him.

"I, we…I…"

"Emma, we're happy for you. Eli is a nice boy. We couldn't have picked someone better for you."

Dad chimed in, "Remember the no closed door rule." He quickly added, "Except when you're changing. It's locked, then."

Mom laughed. Apparently, Dad had clued her in while we were upstairs after all.

I was leaving before this conversation got any worse. "I'm going to bed."

"Good night, hon."

"Goodnight." Waving over my shoulder, I flew up the stairs. Wait until Sarah heard what happened, she wouldn't believe it.

Chapter Thirty-Five

Emma

I woke up to my telephone buzzing. Rolling over, I untangled the sheet from my arm and patted the floor alongside my bed trying to find it.

Good morning, gorgeous. :)

I couldn't stop my cheesy grin. Definitely a nice start to the day. I tucked the pillow more firmly under my head, and propped myself up enough to answer Eli's text.

Good morning! What are you doing up so early?

Waiting to see you.

???

It took a few seconds for his response this time.

Do you feel like going for a drive? I thought we could go over to the Falls, hike a little.

I'd only been there once, with my parents, but I remembered how pretty it was. Trails that wrapped through the woods, natural waterfalls all over. The thought of walking those trails with Eli made me giddy.

I'd LOVE to!!!! When do you want to go???

LOL. How about we leave at 10:00. Will that be enough time for you to get ready?

I glanced at the time. It was almost nine. More than enough time to shower and dress, and grab some breakfast.

Yep! I'll come over as soon as I'm ready, ok?

Sounds good, see you then.

I jumped up in bed, wanting to get started. A minute later, another text came in from him.

Make sure to wear good sneakers or boots!

I rolled my eyes.

Yes, Dad. ;-)

:-p

Laughter bubbled up seeing his message. After I hopped out of bed, I decided I'd better run it by Mom and Dad about going hiking with Eli, though I couldn't imagine they'd mind. They'd never cared before when I did things with him. Although I hadn't been dating him before.

I stopped short. Were we dating? As I went downstairs to find something to eat, I told myself not to worry about labeling whatever we were doing, and just enjoy it.

Mom was already in the kitchen when I got there, standing at the counter pouring a mug of coffee. "Good morning, hon. Did you sleep well?"

I nodded. "Yep. Thanks."

I walked over to the cupboard, opened it, and rooted around for the cereal I liked. I finally found it behind some healthy junk my parents ate. Chocolatey goodness over cardboard in a box, talk about a no-brainer.

Mom leaned against the counter, holding her coffee in two hands, blowing it gently. "So, any plans for today?"

I busied myself pouring cereal into the bowl. "I thought I'd go hiking with Eli up at the falls in a bit."

Mom crossed over to the refrigerator. She got out the milk and handed it to me. "Oh, that sounds fun. I'm sure you'll have a great time."

It couldn't be that easy. I placed the cereal box on the counter, and turned to face her. "Go ahead, say whatever it is you're dying to say." I sighed, waiting for the teasing, or questions, or whatever else she was going to throw at me.

Instead, Mom shook her head, smiling gently. "Hon, I'm not going to say anything negative. I told you last night, I like Eli. And I'm happy for you." She reached out to smooth my hair. "I've known how you felt for a while now, maybe even longer than you."

I blushed, and began to fiddle with my spoon, not meeting her eyes.

"But," she continued, "I still want you to take things slow. Don't rush things, Emma."

"I'm not."

"Okay, good. Just enjoy this time, the newness of it. I know you've known Eli practically your whole life, but this is different."

I finally looked up to meet her gaze. "How did you know? I mean, how did you know things changed with us without me telling you?"

She laughed. "Oh sweetie, you didn't have to say a word. It was written all over your face."

Flushing a little, I tried to hide my grin. I grabbed my bowl and walked over to the table to sit down and eat. Spooning some Pebbles into my mouth, I reached for the orange juice setting on the table to pour a glass.

"Where's Dad?"

"He ran to the hardware store. Apparently he's going to try to fix that loose doorknob in our bathroom."

I raised my eyebrows. "*Dad* is? Dad doesn't even own a screwdriver."

Mom waved her hand. "Well, maybe that's what he went to the hardware store for." She laughed.

The front door opened, and footsteps headed toward the kitchen. Dad came into the room, proudly clutching a brown paper sack with "True Value" written across it in red type.

"I got it!" He proclaimed proudly, holding up the bag. He turned to me. "Morning, sleepyhead!"

I waved my spoon at him. "Morning, Daddy. So, I hear you're going to do some home repairs."

"Yes, I am. I'm going to start with the doorknob, and then I may even try to fix that leak we have in the downstairs bathroom sink."

This would not end well. The last time he tried to repair something plumbing related, we went without water for two days before he caved and finally called a professional. I shook my head but said nothing, shoveling in another spoonful of cereal instead.

Dad exclaimed. "Oh! Emma, I forgot, there's something out on the table in the entryway for you." He smiled teasingly.

"I think you have an admirer. It was outside the door when I came in. I didn't know you were even awake yet."

My pulse quickened. Did Eli leave something for me? "What is it?" I asked, breakfast forgotten.

"Well, go see."

It took every ounce of self-control I possessed to walk at a normal pace. After all, I wanted to be mature about the whole thing. Mom followed, curiosity written all over her face. In the breezeway, I immediately noticed something wrapped in green tissue paper like you get from a florist.

Was it another rose? That meant it *had* to be from Eli, considering yesterday's events. Maybe I was wrong about the first one and that was from him too. I fought back a grin. I removed the card stapled to the paper. Setting it down for a minute, I peeled the tissue paper back to peek inside.

"What is it?" Mom craned her neck to see.

"It's two roses." There was no use trying to hide my excitement now. "Look." I held the pale pink roses out for my mother to inspect too.

She leaned down to smell them, smiling. "Aw, Emma, they're beautiful. Eli has good taste."

"Yeah, he does." I set the flowers down, and began to open the card. *Wait. What if he said something embarrassing?* "I think I'll read this later."

Mom leaned in to kiss my cheek. "That's fine. A girl has the right to read a note from a boy in private." She smiled before she turned and walked back into the kitchen.

I couldn't wait to see what he'd written for me this time. Once I got to my room, I closed the door softly, and then sat at my desk to open the envelope. It held a small white card.

You make me smile.

I grinned, reading his words, as my stomach flip-flopped in delicious excitement. It still seemed unreal that Eli thought of me that way. He'd always been nice to me, but roses? Sweet sayings? It was romantic and unexpected, like something in a movie that you never believe will happen to you. At least I sure hadn't.

It seemed silly to hide the notes now that I knew they were from him. I reached up and pinned the card to the wide corkboard above my desk, next to some of my treasured photos and ticket stubs. Opening my top desk drawer, I pulled out the first note, and pinned that up as well. The sight of them tacked up next to pictures of the two of us made me smile like a fool.

The other rose. It was still in the closet!

I laughed at my senseless hiding spot, and walked over to retrieve it, being careful not to bump it since I didn't want it losing even more petals. I unwrapped the new flowers, and gingerly slipped them into the vase as well. *Perfect.* I couldn't wait to thank him.

Maybe he acted so weird about the first one since I hadn't acknowledged he'd sent it. Completely understandable.

After throwing on a pair of jeans and my favorite Star Wars T-shirt, I sat on the bed to lace up my sneakers. Since I'd never had any use for hiking boots, my beat up Sketchers would have to do. A loose braid seemed like my best bet; less chance of my hair going crazy in the heat that way.

It was almost ten. My stomach fluttered at the thought of seeing Eli, of getting to spend the day hiking with him. I hurried down the stairs.

"Mom! Dad! I'm leaving," I called when I reached the bottom.

Mom poked her head out of the kitchen. "Bye, sweetie, have a good time. Be careful."

"Thanks, I will. See you later."

The warmth hit me immediately when I stepped outside. The sun shone without a cloud in sight. The earthy smell of fresh cut grass carried in the slight breeze as I turned left to head across the lawn toward Eli's house.

When I reached his door, I faltered. Had the rules changed about walking in and out of each other's homes considering the difference in our relationship? I shifted awkwardly from one foot to the other on the front stoop, trying to figure out what to do. Finally deciding to err on the side of caution, I knocked.

After a minute or two, the door swung open.

"Emma! What are you doing knocking? How are you, honey?" Eli's mom stood in the entrance, a wide smile on her face. Her hazel eyes crinkled up at each corner.

"I'm doing good, Mrs. Perry. How are you?"

"Busy, busy. You know me." She smiled, and opened the door wider. "Come on in. Eli's upstairs. He told me you two were going hiking today." She wiped her hands on the bright artist's smock tied around her ample waist. She had the same dark hair as her son, and wore it flowing loose over her shoulders.

I stepped inside, and a welcome coolness washed over me. I glanced toward the stairs.

"You can go on up if you like. He should be ready any minute." She motioned toward the steps. "Go ahead, I'm working on a new piece, anyway."

"Okay, thanks."

She gave a small wave before turning to head down the hallway that led to her studio at the back of the house.

I hurried up the stairs. Did I have the nerve to kiss him when I thanked him for the flowers? I crossed the hall at the top of the stairs to go to the second door on the right. Eli's room.

His door was open. He sat on his bed, bent over at the waist, tying the red laces on his hiking boots. He wore earbuds, and moved his head in time to whatever he was listening to.

I walked over and poked him on the shoulder.

He jerked upright, a broad smile crossing his face when he saw me. "Hey!" He reached out, pulling me down on his lap. I laughed, putting my arm across his back to keep from toppling over. He tugged the earbuds out with one hand.

I decided to go for it before I lost my nerve. Leaning in, I gave him a quick kiss on the lips. He looked surprised for a second, then kissed me back, longer than my little peck. As much as I liked the kiss, I pulled back after a few seconds, worried his mom would walk in and see us.

"Hi." I smiled.

"Hmm…I like this kind of greeting." He nuzzled my neck.

I giggled, pushing him away. "I wanted to say thank you."

"You're welcome. Though if I had known you liked hiking this much, I definitely would have asked you sooner." He wiggled his eyebrows.

Laughing, I wrapped my arms around his neck. "No, silly. For the flowers. They're beautiful. It was so sweet of you."

His brows knitted together.

My smile faltered.

He shifted sideways on the bed, moving me off his lap to sit next to him.

"What's wrong?" A sinking feeling began to fill me.

"What flowers?" he asked carefully.

Uneasiness crept in. Maybe he was teasing me.

"The…the flowers you left for me on my porch." His lips pressed together, and I could see the pulse on the side of his forehead begin to throb.

Oh no, they weren't from him. What words could I possibly use to backpedal from this completely awkward situation?

I prayed that any minute he would jump up, smiling, and yell, "Gotcha!"

He didn't.

"I didn't leave you flowers," he said. "I thought when I saw it that maybe your parents gave it to you. For Easter or something, I don't know. They've given you flowers before, and you certainly didn't mention it the other night when I was over."

I opened my mouth, then immediately closed it again.

He stood up so abruptly, I almost fell off the bed. He walked across the room, pushing his hair back on his head with both hands. Spinning back around to face me, he looked hurt. And upset.

"So let me get this straight. *Jake* gave it to you?"

"Eli, no. Well, I don't know. I thought they were from you." I stood as well, walking over to him, arms outstretched.

He moved away, holding up his hands. "Don't." He took a few more steps. "Why would he send you flowers? I thought nothing happened between you two. He must really have a thing for you to send you flowers." He practically spit out the words.

"It didn't. I don't know. From the cards, I just thought…" I was making things worse.

"What cards? He sent you cards, too?" He shoved his hands in and out of his pockets and paced, not meeting my eyes.

"No. Well yes, but they were with the roses."

That got him to look at me. "Roses? *Plural*" He looked incredulous. "So he sent you more?"

I nodded. "This morning. There were two," I whispered.

He shook his head, looking stunned.

"Eli, please, forget I said anything."

"How the hell am I supposed to forget some guy sent you roses the day after you were kissing *me*?"

I began to get mad, too. It wasn't my fault, I didn't send the damn things. Apparently the day was a complete waste of good lip gloss.

"I don't know…forget it." I took a deep breath, willing myself to calm down. "Eli, I honestly didn't know they were from him, and now that I do, I'll get rid of them. Okay?

You're what matters to me." I begged him with my eyes to understand, to believe me. "*You.* Only you."

He sighed, and walked back over to the bed to sit down. I sat beside him, tentatively reaching out my hand and placing it on his leg. "I didn't know," I repeated.

He hung his head a moment. "I know. It's not your fault."

The anger faded from his face, replaced with resignation. He shook his head, finally looking up at me. "It really took me by surprise, I guess." He shrugged. "I shouldn't have acted like that, I'm sorry."

He reached his hand up and laid it across mine. "So what did they say?"

"What?"

"The cards, what did they say?"

"Eli, it doesn't matter. Can't we forget all of this?"

He shook his head. "Em, I need to know. Please."

I sighed. There was no way I wanted to lie to him; lies were what caused all the problems in the first place. I looked right at him. "The first one just said, 'You're beautiful,' and the one today said, 'You make me smile.'"

He looked pained.

I shifted, taking his hand in both of mine. "But Eli, none of that matters to me. I don't care what the cards said."

"But that's just it, Em. You should. You *should* be told those things, except I should have been the one telling you. And I didn't." He looked away. "And I'm sorry I didn't."

Not sure how to answer that, I simply laid my head on his shoulder. He reached up and stroked my hair, not speaking for a moment.

"I'm going to stop taking you for granted, Em. I want to show you how incredible I think you are. I want you to know how I see you, all you mean to me."

"I do know," I said softly.

"No, you don't. Because I never really showed you, but I

will. You just wait and see. I promise you that."

The rest of the day was amazing, and turned out to *not* be a waste of good lip gloss.

He'd brought his camera, and we took turns snapping pictures of each other posing in front of the different waterfalls. Some were silly—making whacky faces or standing like an ostrich, while others were normal, just smiling for each other. We even tried a few with both of us in the frame, Eli holding the camera out as far as he could and then yelling, "Cheese!" He was nuts. And awesome. And just so much fun to spend the day with.

Hunger pains hit by about 1:00, and since we passed Roma on the way back, we decided to stop there to grab some lunch.

After placing our order for a medium pie with ham and pineapple, we decided to play a game in the back until the server brought our food out.

I'd scored my third point in air hockey and cheered when a voice spoke behind me.

"She's good, isn't she?"

My hand froze on the paddle, the excitement from a moment ago forgotten. I looked at Eli. He stood at the opposite end of the table, jaw clenched.

Jake walked around me to stand alongside the table. "I mean, we only played about, what was it, Emma? Five or six games that night?"

Paste. My mouth was made of paste. Nothing came out. I looked back and forth between the two guys, wishing desperately for a sink hole to appear under me and swallow me up, but of course I didn't get that lucky.

Jake smiled again, like he didn't have a care in the world. He walked over to Eli, holding out his hand. "Hi. It's Ellie, right?"

Eli refused to acknowledge Jake's outstretched hand. "Eli," he corrected stiffly.

"Oh, that's right, sorry about that, man." Jake dropped his hand when it became apparent that Eli wasn't about to shake it.

"Am I interrupting?" Jake feigned innocence, looking from Eli to me.

"We're playing a game while we wait for our food," I said weakly.

"Oh, I'm sorry. Well, I won't keep you." Jake began to walk toward the archway leading out of the game room. As he passed me, he stopped, lightly placing his hand on my upper arm. He leaned in and whispered loudly, "I hope you liked the roses I sent you." He squeezed my arm gently before continuing out the door.

I looked up at Eli, who stood at the other end of the table, paddle forgotten in his hand. He looked ready to spit. I dropped my paddle and hurried toward him.

"I'm sorry. I had no way of knowing he would be here."

He shook his head. "I'm not mad at you, Em. It's him. What a dick."

I stood next to him, silently agreeing. I didn't understand why Jake acted that way, it seemed so out of character from the Jake I knew.

"I mean, who the hell does he think he is? He did that on purpose. And you went out with that guy? Seriously?"

"I know you don't want to hear it, but he didn't act like that with me. I don't know what that was all about."

He snorted. "I'll tell you what it was all about; it was him trying to make sure I knew that he wasn't backing down."

I sighed. "Eli, you're right. He acted like a jerk. But what he does is on him." I bit my lip. "I'll talk to him, explain things."

He shook his head. "Yeah, good luck with that."

Chapter Thirty-Six

Emma

Later that night, I showered and changed into some comfy pajamas. We'd headed back to my house right after our pizza, but then Eli went home, explaining that he had to help with some work around the house, and would call me later. I hoped he wasn't still upset about the Jake thing.

I took a seat at my desk and twisted my hair absently while I waited for my laptop to boot up. Clicking over to Facebook, I realized I should probably delete Kelli's profile, since there was no reason to keep it up. Just seeing it made me feel kind of stupid. I cringed thinking of all the messages I'd sent to Eli without having any idea he knew it was me, and wished I'd had the guts to simply tell him the truth in the first place.

After deleting it, I logged into my own account, scrolling through my home page. About halfway down, I spied a picture of myself standing in front of a waterfall, laughing. It was from our hike. The time stamp showed Eli had posted it about two hours ago. He'd written, *The most beautiful girl I know.*

My eyes misted up. I recognized it as his way of telling me that he was proud to be with me, that I mattered to him.

I typed a single symbol in the comment box, and pressed enter.

<3

A simple heart. It was my way of acknowledging his gesture, and thanking him.

I walked over to my futon and flipped idly through a catalogue. I needed to call Jake. Granted, he'd acted like a jerk at the restaurant, but he'd always been nice to me before that. Sighing, I reached over and picked up the phone. I would explain things to him, and hopefully he'd understand. He answered on the third ring.

"Hello?"

"Hi, Jake. It's Emma." Silence. "Jake? You there?"

"I'm here," he answered. "What's up?"

I cleared my throat. What was I supposed to say? *Oh, sorry I used you and then thought I might have liked you but I'm with Eli now?* I settled for, "I wanted to say I'm sorry if I did anything to upset you. And, I shouldn't have acted the way I did with you. You know, before." I paused.

The silence returned.

"I was confused, and I'll admit, you were really sweet, and…" I trailed off, not having a clue what else to say that would make me sound less stupid.

"So the plan worked, huh? You two are together?"

"Yes. We are," I said softly.

"Well, that's great. I'm glad I could help."

"Jake, I'm honestly sorry. You're a really great guy, you are. It's just—"

"I'm not him," he interrupted flatly.

I didn't answer. After all, what could I say? No, he wasn't.

"Look, Emma, I have to go. But I hope things work out

for you." His voice softened. "I mean that, you deserve it."

"Thank you." This was harder than I'd expected.

"Well, I guess I'll see you around sometime."

"Yeah, maybe I'll see you around," I echoed quietly.

"Bye, Emma."

"Bye, Jake," I whispered.

I felt awful. Jake had been nothing but sweet. I hadn't meant to, but I knew that I'd completely used him. First to make Eli jealous, and then to fill a void. It'd been flattering hearing someone say the things he did, and look at me the way he did.

But it'd always been Eli I really wanted. I knew that now with complete certainty.

Setting the phone down next to me, I leaned back and closed my eyes. At least it was done.

Chapter Thirty-Seven

Eli

"So what are you thinking about?"

I reached over to grab Emma's hand, and when she smiled up at me, something inside me shifted. I didn't think I'd ever get tired of her smile.

She shook her head. "Actually, nothing. It feels nice to be here with you."

My grin grew wider and I traced a pattern with my thumb on the inside of her wrist. I shifted slightly on the blanket, moving closer. Her breathing hitched a little as I leaned in, and it drove me crazy. Everything about her turned me on.

I dropped a light kiss on her lips and leaned back to look at her. Her hair curled around her head where she lay, spilling over her shoulders. I hooked a finger under the strap of the little white sundress she wore; her skin felt like satin. I pressed my lips to her shoulder and then grinned when she giggled. Movie people couldn't have written a better day. Tree branches above us were starting to bloom, tiny white buds bursting from the dark wood. The air smelled of fresh grass and grilled food

We packed a picnic lunch to bring along to Stoyer's Dam. Emma had wanted to feed the ducks, and after that, we spread out a blanket underneath some dogwood trees and listened to music and read together for a while.

We also talked for hours. We talked through everything that'd happened. She opened up about how scared she'd been to let me know that she was interested, and I apologized for taking her for granted and being so stupid and it taking me as long as it had to realize how I felt. I felt closer to her than I'd ever felt before.

As much as I loved looking at Emma, my stomach was starting to protest. I sat up somewhat regretfully. "Are you hungry yet?"

"Not really, are you?"

"A little." My stomach grumbled just then, making us both laugh.

"Well here." She reached in the cooler to grab a small sub and a can of soda and handed it to me. "You don't have to wait for me, silly." She flashed me another smile before lying back down. "Go ahead and eat."

"I'd rather do this." I slowly leaned down, bending over her, and touched her lips softly. In just a moment, the kiss turned deeper. When she responded, her touch felt like the electric sensation before a rainstorm. I shivered.

I grinned between kisses when the book in her hand dropped to the blanket, forgotten.

Loud giggles brought us both back to earth. Emma sat up, a sheepish expression on her face. We both looked around to see two young girls, maybe eleven or so, standing about ten feet away from us next to their bikes. They leaned in to each other, whispering and still giggling as they watched us.

I sat up as well. "Talk about timing."

Emma cleared her throat. "It seems we have an audience. Um, maybe we should eat."

Laughing, I snagged the sub from the blanket, unwrapped it, and handed her half. "We'll pick up later where we left off." I winked.

She shook her head, laughing. "Deal."

Chapter Thirty-Eight

Emma

Spring break went by way too quickly. Eli and I spent a lot of time together, and things seemed to be going better than I could have hoped. I worried that coming back to school after break might feel awkward, with all our classmates seeing us together, but it turned out I worried for nothing. Whenever he'd run into me between classes, he always made a point of coming up for a quick kiss, or to just squeeze my hand before rushing off again.

I'd talked to Sarah about it. Her big advice was that I needed to stop worrying so much and just go with it. She pointed out, "You guys pretty much have the same relationship you always did. Only now there's kissing involved."

Laughing, I had to admit she was sort of right.

I still ate lunch with my friends, and Eli still ate with Kevin and his soccer crew. For one, I didn't want Sarah to feel like a third wheel since Doug ate lunch a different period. Plus, it was important to me to still have girl time, too. But Eli and I always met up to walk to our lockers after lunch.

We'd just finished lunch about a week after coming back from spring break when the bell rang and Eli materialized next to me.

"Hey, gorgeous." He smiled down at me.

Sarah made a show of gagging when he leaned down to kiss me. "You two lovebirds need to get a room," she said, smiling.

"Oh you know we love you, too." Eli looped an arm around her shoulder as we walked to our lockers. He looked at me and winked. He was adorable.

After we rounded the corner, we all stopped short, and Sarah squealed at the top of her lungs.

White paper roses decorated the edges of her locker, with the word, PROM? spelled out in large red construction paper letters down the center. Doug stood next to the locker wearing a top hat and a giant smile.

Sarah ran up to him and threw herself at him. He could probably take that as a *yes*.

I misted up a bit. I wanted to be happy for my friend, but I also felt…jealous. Eli hadn't said a word about going. I knew he hated dances, always had, but I'd been dropping some hints, hoping he'd make an exception. He hadn't taken the bait.

He glanced down at me. "I'm glad you're not into that kind of lame crap." He could barely hold back his laughter, like he found the whole thing so hilarious.

I nodded. "Yeah. Totally lame." I pasted on a wobbly smile as we headed to class and I tried to tell myself it was no big deal.

It seemed like forever until the dismissal bell rang. I was

supposed to be meeting Eli in front of the school, since he was giving me a ride home. I shaded my eyes as I peered across the steps and pick-up area, searching for him, but he wasn't anywhere in sight.

Walking down the steps, I wondered if I'd somehow gotten it wrong, and was supposed to meet him inside at one of our lockers. I decided to wait a few minutes before going back in to look for him. Maybe he got held up talking to one of his teachers.

I leaned against a brick column at the bottom of the steps to wait. It'd been a long day, and between everyone talking about the Prom and a pop quiz in science, my mood sucked. I sighed.

Right as I looked up to check the door again, Carissa sashayed down the steps without her usual posse for once. As if she felt my gaze, she glanced up and zoned directly in on me. Her china-doll face immediately morphed into something ugly. With a determined glare, she marched straight up to me until she stood only inches away.

"So, I hear Eli took the pity route," she remarked snidely.

I turned my head, but she wasn't so easily put off.

"Yeah, I heard from a *very* good source that he felt sorry for you after you posted some fake profile just to try to get him." She snickered. "Wow, talk about desperation."

"I don't know what you're talking about," I said. "And sorry to burst your bubble, but *he* asked *me* out, not the other way around."

Carissa laughed, eyes glinting. "*Right.* Was that before or after you were pathetic enough to pretend you were someone else, and had some other guy pretend to date you?" She shook her head, pushing pouty lips out in a mock frown. "I mean, I have to say, that was truly sad…even for you."

Spinning to face her, I burst out, "What *exactly* is your problem?"

Carissa widened her eyes. "I don't know what you mean. I don't have a problem. I was just telling you what everyone in school's been saying." She shrugged. "Sorry if the truth hurts." The evil grin returned.

If Carissa knew, then everyone knew. Gossip to Carissa was like pure crystal to a meth-head—she couldn't resist it.

"You know, Carissa, for years you've gone out of your way to treat me like shit every single chance you got. That might make a person wonder what was driving you to act that way." I took a step closer. "And you know what? I think I've finally figured it out. You can't stand seeing what Eli and I have."

She rolled her eyes. "Whatever."

But I was on a roll. I knew I was being horrible, but couldn't stop myself. Too many years of taking her crap had brought me to that exact point in time.

"No, that's it. Even before Eli and I got together, we still had more than you've *ever* had with anyone. Everyone at school is afraid of you because they know what a two-faced vindictive bitch you are, and they don't want to get on your bad side. But the truth is, no one actually even *likes* you."

Carissa's eyes narrowed, and her face grew stony.

It felt good to finally let it all out. "People might be nice to your face, and jump when you say jump, but it's not because they're your friends. It's only because they don't trust you." I scoffed. "You knew you couldn't have the one person you wanted. *Eli.* You lost your shot with him. And you're flat out jealous that I have him in a way you *never* will."

I flew backward as Carissa screamed and lunged at me.

"What the hell are you doing?" I yelled, trying to push her away. "Are you freaking insane?"

Carissa stopped and released the hold she had on my shirt, as if she suddenly realized where she was and what she was doing. Her normally perfect hair flew wild around her mottled face. She sniffed and smoothed it down, looking around the landing at the group of students staring in our direction. "You're not worth it," she sneered. "You're a nobody." She wheeled away.

Heart pounding, I couldn't believe what she'd just done. The other students continued to stare over at me with interest, having witnessed the whole show. It was sure to make the gossip rounds by tomorrow.

Lifting my chin, I adjusted the top of my shirt that had slipped down my shoulder when Carissa shoved me, and marched away. A few kids whispered or snickered as I passed. I refused to look anywhere but straight ahead.

As I crossed the street near the student parking area, a voice called my name. Eli's voice. My first instinct was to simply ignore him, but when he called a second time, I finally turned around, my face expressionless.

"Em! What are you doing?" Lines furrowed in his forehead. "I saw you headed this way and ran to try to catch up to you." He noticed my face. "What's wrong?" He took a step toward me, his concern clear.

"What's wrong?" The words came out eerily calm. "Why don't you ask your good friend Carissa?"

Confusion washed over his features. "What are you talking about? What happened?"

My expressionless mask broke, and I lost it. "Carissa just attacked me, *after* humiliating me in front of everyone standing out front waiting for the buses."

Shock replaced the confusion. "She *what*? Why?"

I stared at him. "*Why?* What's that supposed to mean? Like I did something to prompt it?"

He shook his head. Reaching out, he took my hand. "No. I'm sorry. I didn't mean it the way it sounded. Are you okay?"

I pulled away. "I'm fine. It was more embarrassing than anything."

Eli looked livid. "I don't care. She can't go around doing this. You have to report her."

"No! I'm not going and telling on her."

He closed his eyes a moment. "Fine. So what did she say, anyway?"

"She informed me how she knew all about the profile I put on Facebook, and told me how you're just going out with me out of pity." I stared down at the gravel.

"Oh, Em. No. Come here." He reached out and pulled me into his arms, holding me tight. At first I resisted, but after a few seconds I collapsed into him, sobbing.

"I was so humiliated. Everyone heard her. Everyone thinks I'm this big pathetic loser."

"Sh…It's okay," he soothed, stroking my hair while pulling me even closer. "Nobody thinks that. I don't think that."

I hiccupped through my tears. "Carissa does."

"Who cares what she thinks? Carissa's a loser." He pulled back a little so I could see his face. "You're worth one hundred Carissas, and she knows it." He smiled down at me, his familiar smile that I loved so much, and wiped a tear away as it slipped down my cheek.

"I think she still likes you. Would you rather go out with her?"

He stared at me. "Em, how could you even think that?" He shook his head. "Not in a million years. Don't you get it? *You* are the only girl I want."

"But…but why did you tell her?" My eyes welled up again; I couldn't help it.

Eli shook his head. "I didn't tell her." He sighed. "The only thing I can think is that Kevin said something to her. I told him about it when everything was all weird between us and we were fighting. I needed someone to talk to." He closed his eyes for a second. "I'm so sorry. And trust me, I'm going to talk to Kevin about opening his big mouth. I'm so sorry," he repeated.

I could tell he felt awful, and knew it wasn't his fault. I understood needing to talk to a friend; after all, I'd told Sarah. I wiped another tear away. "I know she's going to go around telling everyone you feel sorry for me. And maybe I shouldn't care at all, but I can't help it."

He leaned in and kissed me tenderly. "Em, I promise you, no one is going to doubt how I feel about you, including Carissa."

The sniffles were back. "You don't know that."

He smiled, eyes loving. "Trust me, okay?"

Looking into his eyes, I did trust him. He'd never lied to me. Nodding, I said, "Okay," but I didn't really see how he could really make things better…even if he wanted to.

He reached for my hand once again, accompanied by a gentle smile. "Can I give you a ride now?"

I nodded. "I'm sorry I got so freaked out."

"It's okay, don't worry about it. I told you before, I'm here for you." He brought my hand up to his mouth and kissed it. "And I meant it."

We walked across the student lot to his car, and hopped in. As I closed the door, he looked my way and smiled. "Things will seem better tomorrow, I promise."

I didn't see how that would happen, but didn't really want to dwell on it. So instead, I nodded. "I know." Too bad I didn't believe my own words.

Chapter Thirty-Nine

Emma

Eli didn't call me later that night. Instead, he sent a quick text about 9:00 telling me goodnight and that he would see me at school the next day.

Sleep was hard to come by that night. Everything kept running through my head over and over no matter how much I kept telling myself I was being ridiculous. I'd liked Eli for so long that it was hard for me to really believe all my wishes were coming true with him. But yet I knew he had my back no matter what.

Sarah told me the same thing on the phone earlier when I'd called her to talk about it. "Em, you need to trust him. Carissa loves drama, period. And if she can mess with your head, all the better in her mind. Don't let her."

Eli was right. Sarah was right. Carissa wasn't worth it. What we had was real, and I wasn't going to doubt him…or *myself* for that matter…anymore, because of her. Life was for living, not for giving in to bullies.

I barely saw him the next day in school. He waited by my locker in the morning, giving a rushed explanation that he had to finish some project, kissed me and took off. He wasn't at lunch either. And on top of that, several of his friends seemed to be giving me funny looks, or would stop talking as soon as I came within earshot.

I was ready for the day to be over. Finally, the dismissal bell rang. Grabbing the books I needed for homework out of my locker, I slammed it shut, looking around hoping to see him in the hall. He was nowhere around. Sighing, I headed to catch the bus home.

I'd just pushed open the double doors that led outside when Sarah stopped me.

"Wait! Emma."

I turned. "Hey, what's up?"

She stood inside the door. "Um, do you have the history notes?"

I stared at her. "Sarah, we don't even have History together. What's up?"

She stood, trying not to laugh.

"What's so funny?"

She only shook her head, then pointed past my shoulder.

Spinning around, I still didn't see anything. Then Kevin appeared, stepping around the side of the door, and handed me a yellow rose. Perplexed, I just looked at him. "Uh, what's this for?"

Sarah giggled behind me, but neither of them said a word. Instead, they pointed down the crowded steps that led to the bus landing.

Completely confused now, I asked, "*What*?"

"Just go down," Sarah hissed, a grin breaking out.

What in the world?

I turned and walked down. Halfway to the bottom, a guy I recognized from Eli's softball team stepped over to me, and pulled another yellow rose from behind his back, handing it to me. He also pointed for me to continue down. By this time, other students standing around were watching curiously.

As I stood on the final step, Megan walked out of the crowd milling at the bottom to hand me a third rose.

I was completely lost. What the heck was going on? Eli had to be behind this somehow, but I didn't see him anywhere.

All of a sudden, music blared from somewhere close by. Pink's "Perfect" began to play. I stopped dead, looking around.

The crowd broke apart, and about ten students across from me on the bus landing started doing some choreographed dance in time to the music, pointing and staring straight at me, smiles wide. Most of them were friends of Eli's from his teams. It was unreal, these jocks gyrating and twirling…they were actually pretty good. I laughed and waved to them.

Kids began hooting and cheering. Right before it got to the chorus, I felt someone walk around me from behind.

Eli moved to stand in front of me, wearing a suit jacket over his jeans and T-shirt. He held a dozen red roses in his hand. He was grinning. "I told you to trust me," he whispered.

My eyes were ready to pop out of my head as I stared at him. He looked absolutely gorgeous holding that huge mass of roses. For me. Tears threatened.

He handed me the flowers, and began to sing, even if it was a little off-tune.

"*Pretty pretty please, will you go to prom with me? I've known you since the first grade. You were my best friend. Pretty pretty please, will you go to prom with me? You are perfect, you are perfect to me.*"

A group of guys from his soccer team held up a huge banner that read, *Prom??* with hearts all around the letters.

I burst into tears.

Everyone clapped and cheered around us. Eli stood before me, eyes never leaving my face, smiling just for me.

Finally, I realized that I'd never even answered him. There was no way I could form a coherent word, so I nodded, *yes*.

Eli moved in and grabbed my face in his hands, kissing me in a way that left absolutely no room for doubt for me or anyone watching that he meant it.

The catcalls got even louder. Sarah and Megan were suddenly there too, laughing and hugging us both.

I wiped tears from my eyes, laughing and trying to catch my breath all at once. "How did you do this?" I couldn't believe it. I hadn't seen it coming in a million years. Looking around at everyone standing on the steps, or down on the landing in front of us, I was completely overwhelmed. It was like that scene that you don't believe ever really happens in real life. I noticed Carissa standing off to the side, head down. She looked like she'd given up. I actually felt a little sorry for her. But just a little.

He pushed his bangs out of his eyes, laughing along with me. "I told you yesterday I had a project to finish. This is what I've been working on for the last week or so." He leaned in to brush away one of my tears. His kaleidoscope eyes smiled down on me.

I held my hand to my heart; it was going double-time, and I was sure it was going to explode out of my chest any second. "This is just…Omigod." I reached up and hugged him, crushing the roses between us. "Thank you so much." I couldn't stop crying.

"So you liked it?" He brushed a curl out of my eye where the wind blew it across my face.

"You have no idea. I *loved* it." I still couldn't believe he did this. "But you hate dances. I didn't think you'd want to go."

He shook his head, gazing at me in wonder. "Em, don't you get it? I may not like dances, but…" He paused, then softly caressed my cheek with his thumb, never losing eye contact. "That doesn't matter," he continued softly, speaking just for me, "because I love *you*."

I couldn't breathe.

Bending his head slowly toward me, he repeated, "I love you, Emma," before he kissed me, an amazing, perfect, fairytale ending kiss. My head spun; it was like a dream, except I knew it wasn't, because somewhere I could still hear clapping and cheering and music around us.

I pulled back from the kiss, just long enough to whisper, "I love you, too."

The next time we kissed, everything faded but him. His touch. The feel of his heart beating against mine. And I knew everything really *was* perfect, just like our song.

Acknowledgments

There are so many people I owe massive appreciation for making this book a reality. First, a world of thanks goes to my daughter, Hope, for putting up with the many nights of leftovers and takeout while I finished "Just one more round of edits." To my son, Corey—you have so much talent that you inspire me daily to do better. To my amazing CP, Carey Torgesen, thank you from the bottom of my heart. Your constant encouragement and wise feedback mean everything to me. You truly are my soul sister. Abby, you've cheered me on and believed in me through this whole crazy process. I love you so much. Mom and Dad, thank you for teaching me to always follow my dreams. To Kristi Cook and Ella Hort, for loving this story from the first time you read it. To my amazing editor, Alethea, thank you for putting up with me when my nerves would frazzle, and for believing in me in the first place. And to all of my readers, thank you from the bottom of my heart for joining me on this crazy ride—may you all know love, laughter, and amazing memories with your own boy next door.

About the Author

Jodie's writing has been featured on several websites and publications. She received her B.S. in Secondary Education-English from Penn State University and taught for several years before turning to her first love—writing. She lives in a small town in Pennsylvania with her daughter, and adores chocolate, rainy days, and of course devouring as many books as she can get her hands on. She loves to hear from her readers, you can find her online at www.jodieandrefski.net.

CPSIA information can be obtained
at www.ICGtesting.com
Printed in the USA
LVOW08s1631151116
513059LV00001BA/52/P